BLACK INDIANS

Diana Fletcher lived with the Kiowa Nation.

William Loren Katz

BLACK
INDIANS
A HIDDEN HERITAGE

Simon Pulse

New York   London   Toronto   Sydney

To friends Jean Bond, Alice Walker, Chief Osceola Townsend, George Tooks, and the late Woody Strode. And to Kenneth Wiggins Porter, forerunner, scholar, mentor, who embraced the creed lived by Wild Cat and John Horse—love of people and resistance to tyranny.

PICTURE CREDITS

Western History Collections, University of Oklahoma Library: Frontis, 161, 167; Division of Manuscripts, University of Oklahoma Library: 166; The Denver Public Library, Western History Collection: 6, 182, 183; Library of Congress: 17, 105, 128; Bibliotèque Nationale, Paris: 36, 38, 41, 134; Chicago Historical Society: 94; Minnesota Historical Society (C. A. Zimmerman, photographer): 121; Nevada State Historical Society: 124; Glenn Shirley Western Collection: 164. All other prints and photographs are from the author's private collection.

SIMON PULSE
An imprint of Simon & Schuster Children's Publishing Division
1230 Avenue of the Americas, New York, NY 10020

Text copyright © 1986 by Ethrac Publications, Inc.

Designed by Suzanne Haldane
The text of this book was set in Times Roman.
Manufactured in the United States of America

First Aladdin Paperbacks edition January 1997
First Simon Pulse edition December 2005

16 18 20 19 17

The Library of Congress has cataloged the hardcover edition as follows:
Katz, William Loren.
Black Indians.
Bibliography: p. 191. Includes Index.
Summary: Traces the history of relations between blacks and American Indians, from the earliest foreign landings through pioneer days.
ISBN-13: 978-0-689-31196-3 (hc.)
ISBN-10: 0-689-31196-6 (hc.)
1. Afro-Americans—Relations with Indians—Juvenile literature. 2. Indians of North America—Mixed bloods—Juvenile literature. [1. Afro-Americans—Relations with Indians. 2. Indians of North America—Mixed bloods.] I. Title.
E98.R28K37 1986 970.004'043 85-28770
ISBN-13: 978-0-689-80901-9 (pbk.)
ISBN-10: 0-689-80901-8 (pbk.)

The European is to the other races of mankind what man himself is to the lower animals: he makes them subservient to his use and when he cannot subdue he destroys them.

Alexis de Tocqueville, *Democracy in America*, 1835

One of the longest unwritten chapters in the history of the United States is that treating of the relations of the Negroes and the Indians. The Indians were already here when the white men came and the Negroes brought in soon after to serve as a subject race found among the Indians one of their means of escape.

Carter G. Woodson, *Journal of Negro History*, 1920

In the course of time the American people got into Florida and began to live. This caused trouble. The colored people and the Indians, being natives of the land, naturally went on the warpath. They fought until the American people called for peace. The Indians and the Negroes gave them peace.

Joe Philips, Black Seminole, 1930

CONTENTS

Preface to the Paperback Edition

At the Congress of Angostura in 1819, liberator Simon Bolivar was elected president of Venezuela and planned a strategy that would free the Americans of European domination. He also found it necessary to clarify America's racial heritage: "It is impossible to say to which human family we belong. The larger part of the Native population has disappeared, Europeans have mixed with the Indians and the Negroes, and Negroes have mixed with the Indians. We were all born of one mother America, though our fathers had different origins, and we all have differently colored skins. This dissimilarity is of the greatest significance."

Bolivar's insight is still revelation to most Americans. *Black Indians,* designed for schools and young adult readers, immediately stirred adult controversy. Reading it on New York City subways, radio talk show host Gary Bird was confronted by people upset by its cover, topic, and title. Looking at the title, one infuriated rider shouted, "There were *not!*"

In its first four years *Black Indians* inspired two radio documentaries, four TV programs, two magazine cover stories, numerous media interviews, the (Lenga Tooks) song "Black Indian Woman," and book parties at Harlem's Schomburg Center for Research in Black Culture. It led to the creation of Black Indian research organizations in California and New York. In 1990 Abdul Salaam's Brooklyn Academy of Music ballet, *Pee Dee River Bonding,* based on pages 22–26, "had the audience cheering and leaping to its feet," reported the *New York Times*. In John Sayles' brilliant 1996 movie, *Lone Star,* a leading character creates a museum devoted to the Black Seminole story, as it appears in chapters 4–6.

For many families, it struck a mother vein of fond ancestral tales. Ripples of recognition and wonder reached me weekly as readers wanted to talk, share recollections and pictures.

But *Black Indians* also raised difficult issues that it lacked the space to answer. Its title stirred controversy among people with African ancestors who had long accepted themselves as Indians. It raised concerns among

Native Americans still battling a government that traditionally seizes any excuse (e.g., mixture with Africans) to violate treaties, land claims, and human rights (pages 126–130). I hope others will address these vital issues.

The 1920s estimate that a third of African Americans have Indian blood (page 3) requires new research. Today just about every African-American family tree has an Indian branch. Europeans forcefully entered the African blood stream, but Native Americans and Africans merged by choice, invitation, and love. This profound difference cannot be understated—and it explains why families who share this biracial inheritance feel so much solace and pride.

My hope that this first effort would lead to further investigation and synthesis has been met. Its most eloquent testimony is Alice Walker's towering *Temple of My Familiar* in which Fanny becomes fascinated by Seminole Chief John Horse (chapters 5 and 6). Suwelo, her husband, gives Fanny *Black Indians* for her birthday, and when she finishes it, asks her, "What do you love about these people?" Fanny answers:

"I dunno," she said. "They open doors inside me. It's as if they're keys. To rooms inside myself. I find a door inside and it's as if I hear a humming from behind it, and then I get inside somehow, with the key the old ones give me, and are, and as I stumble about in the darkness of the room, I begin to feel the stirring in myself, the humming of the room, and my heart starts to expand with the absolute feeling of bravery, or love, or audacity, or commitment. It becomes a light, and that light enters me, by osmosis, and a part of me that was not clear before is clarified. I radiate this expanded light. Happiness."

And *that*, Suwelo knew, was called "being in love."[1]

Almost two centuries after Simon Bolivar's simple truth, book and author are honored by the inspired use of its findings, and deeply touched by the love expressed by some of its readers.

William Loren Katz, 1996

---

[1]Alice Walker, *The Temple of My Familiar* (New York: Harcourt Brace Jovanovich, 1989), p. 186 (reprinted with permission).

INTRODUCTION

Black Indians? The very words make most people shake their heads in disbelief or smile at what appears to be a joke, a play on words. No one remembers any such person in a school text, history book, or western novel. None ever appeared.

Yet they lived and roamed all over the Americas. Their story began with the first European landings in the New World, reached from New England to Brazil, and continues today. The number of Afro-Americans with an Indian ancestor was once estimated at about one third of the total. In Latin America the percentage is much higher. This means that an important page in history has been missing.

Three great races—red, white, and black—built the Americas together. Their contributions and their interrelationships have filled libraries with scholarly studies, history texts, and novels. The relationship between Europeans and

3

Black Indians of Paraguay.

Native Americans and between Europeans and Africans
have been thoroughly studied.

But one relationship has not. Conspicuous by its neglect
is the relationship on this soil between red and black people.
In 1920 historian Carter G. Woodson called it "one of the
longest unwritten chapters in the history of the United

States." He wondered if Africans did not find "among Indians one of their means to escape" from slavery.

Dr. Woodson's chapter still remains unwritten, his "escape" theory hardly explored. This book means to tackle both the chapter and the theory.

Black Indians, like other Afro-Americans, have been treated by the writers of history as invisible. Their contributions were denied or handed to others. Where mentioned, their role has been distorted. For example, *The Negro Cowboys*, by Durham and Jones, an otherwise objective study, calls black people who joined the Indians "renegades"—a terrifying term borrowed from Hollywood westerns to describe vicious killers. *The Negro Cowboys* also declares "for every Negro renegade who joined against the white man, a company of Negro soldiers fought the Indians." This single sentence mangles some important history. It understates the number of Black Indians by hundreds of thousands. It also suggests slaves should remain loyal to their owners and praises those who "fought the Indians."

It is not that U.S. chroniclers of the past have failed to see a Black Indian heritage through the eyes of nonwhites, for that is understandable. Almost all were white. What is unforgivable is that some have insisted on seeing past events through the eyes of a slaveholding and Indian-killing class that has been dead for a century or more.

But omission, not distortion, is the far more serious culprit in hiding the story of the Black Indians of the Americas. Observers, not expecting to find Africans among Indians, did not report their presence. For example, artist George Catlin painted a magnificent portrait of Chief Osceola when he and other Seminoles were held captive at Fort Multrie in 1837. Catlin never painted or mentioned that Osceola's personal bodyguard of fifty-five warriors included fifty-two Black Seminoles. Had his artistry captured their presence, he would have contributed vastly to our understanding of anthropology and history.

I have some empathy for this blindness. During research for my book, *The Black West*, I kept unearthing frontier documents and photographs that established a significant

Black Indian presence on the U.S. frontier. I never fully weighed my evidence and *The Black West* gave Black Indians minor attention until the third edition. As my private collection of Indian photographs and documentation piled up, it became clear the subject needed fuller treatment.

Though it is unfamiliar terrain, I have chosen to begin this story at the beginning, with the earliest foreign landings in the Western Hemisphere. This has two advantages. It establishes a Black Indian participation in democratic movements years, decades, or centuries before the American Revolution. It also demonstrates that dark people ignored the boundaries drawn by Europeans in their move from one "country" to another in search of liberty, justice, or a better life.

This unknown American story is deeply rooted in the human currents that shaped our early life. Two parallel institutions joined to create Black Indians: the seizure and

In 1886, these Shoshone Indians were photographed in Reno, Nevada, with their black friend "One Horse Charley."

mistreatment of Indians and their lands and the enslavement of Africans. In their conquest of the New World, Europeans were determined to use both dark peoples. "Ten whites are not enough to watch one Negro," said a Portuguese slave master living in Brazil in 1735. To protect slavery and prevent resistance, Europeans developed brutal methods of control and degrading racial policies.

There is evidence that European genocidal attacks on Indians in the New World may have an additional explanation besides land hunger and greed. Perhaps another reason for eliminating Indians was to prevent their alliance with Africans. Colonial Europeans left evidence aplenty that this was often an overriding fear.

Research into early American history confronts one with some inaccurate traditional assumptions and vocabulary. Columbus, believing he had landed in the East Indies, called the inhabitants "Indians." His error has become so much a part of our language that today even many Native Americans accept it. I have used both designations. However, I have dropped such derisive terms as *half-breed, renegade,* and *tribe* in characterizing Native Americans and Africans. If Europeans came from nations, so too did nonwhites.

I have defined Black Indians as people who have a dual ancestry or black people who have lived for some time with Native Americans. When slaves escaped to the woods and joined or began remote communities, they are called by the Spanish term *maroons*.

In discussing the time when most foreigners in the Americas came from either Europe or Africa, I have used such words as *Spaniard* or *African*. When it is clear they were born in the Western Hemisphere, I then use such terms as *white, black,* or *Afro-American*. I have not designated only U.S. citizens as *Americans* for that broad category belongs to all people of the Americas. Despite their bias, I have had no choice but to accept *Latin America, British Colonies,* and *American Revolution* because other phrases would prove cumbersome or unclear.

Kiowa Indian members of the Baptist church included a mixture of Indians and blacks.

I have been humbled by the awesome task of rejecting bias in so explosively controversial a topic and one peopled with so stormy a set of characters. In this story even the simple question of criminality is open to interpretation. Were those who escaped slavery seeking freedom or breaking the law? Were Black Indian maroon settlements havens of self-determination or conspiracies against the European state? One solution I have adopted has been to offer eyewitness accounts, and to see that the neglected views of Africans and Native Americans are presented.

I have never sought a bland neutrality and have consoled myself that unbiased history has yet to be written in our world. This is a labor of love that has introduced me to many exciting Americans it would have been interesting to meet. I have tried hard to balance opinions, present contrasting views, manage personal feelings, and uncover some truths.

This is a subject that deserves further investigation and synthesis. Clearly people and events described in one chapter, or even a part of one, deserve far greater study. If this effort contributes to those ends, a personal goal will have been reached.

—WILLIAM LOREN KATZ

1

IF YOU KNOW
I HAVE A HISTORY

Today most Black Indians do not live in the forests or on the broad plains of the U.S. Most do not inhabit government reservations set aside for Native Americans any more than most Indians do. To be sure they crowd, for example, the Shinnecock reservation on New York's Long Island. But many more walk the crowded streets of nearby New York City. They are found in abundance in the cement caverns of Boston, Chicago, Denver, New Orleans, Cleveland, and Detroit.

They have made a long march from farms, woods, and ranches to skyscrapers, subways, and ghettoes. Most have arrived with only a faint recollection of their adventurous rural heritage and gallant ancestors. The people they meet in school, at work or play cannot appreciate their background because they know nothing about it.

"If you know I have a history, you will respect me," a Black Indian student told a conference of New York teach-

9

ers two decades ago. Her words still ring true. Those who assume that a people have no history worth mentioning are likely to believe they have no humanity worth defending. An historical legacy strengthens a country and its people. Denying a people's heritage questions their legitimacy.

Citizens celebrate this country's daring break from colonial rule, and rejoice in the plucky Minutemen who challenged the British at Lexington and Concord. But a month before those historic skirmishes on the path to freedom, other Americans were pursuing the same goal. Slaves in Ulster County, New York, planned a massive armed rising. Perhaps they had heard the exciting patriotic talk about liberty and independence. Their liberation plot involved slaves in Kingston, Hurley, Marbletown, and upwards of five hundred Native Americans. Unlike the Minutemen, their shot was not heard around the world, their bold conspiracy never found its way into our history books.

These dark people in Ulster County, like thousands of others mentioned in this book, made their contribution to freedom and to their immediate relatives and friends. But other Black Indians made a contribution to the entire U.S. society that deserves consideration.

On the snowy night of March 5, 1770, Crispus Attucks, a Black Natick Indian, stepped dramatically into U.S. history in Boston. He was the first to fall in the Boston Massacre. Benson J. Lossing, a nineteenth-century historian, transformed Attucks into a Nantucket Indian. To Lossing it seemed wrong to place an Afro-American with Native American blood at the daring first moment of American Independence.

Paul Cuffee, a Dartmouth Indian with African parentage, became a wealthy merchant and shipowner in early Massachusetts. He married Alice Pequit of his mother's Wampanoag nation. But his great interest was in protecting fellow Afro-Americans from discrimination in the U.S. and he became the first black man to sponsor a migration of U.S. blacks to Africa. In 1815, he personally paid for and led thirty-eight settlers aboard his ship, *Traveller*, to Sierra Leone. Cuffe became the father of black back-to-Africa movements in this country.

Frederick Douglass, a slave runaway, with mixed African, Indian, and white ancestry, became the leading voice of black America during the Civil War era and the decades that followed. His creed, "If there is no struggle, there is no progress," has inspired reform and revolutionary movements ever since. Douglass's name and accomplishments now adorn most history texts.

Langston Hughes, poet laureate of African-Americans, liked to trace his family tree back to Pocahontas. In that tree also was a man who joined John Brown's famous raid on Harper's Ferry and another who became a Virginia congressman. Hughes, a prolific writer of poetry, plays, short stories, novels, autobiographies, and newspaper columns, became the proud voice of Harlem, New York's black community.

Langston Hughes, photographed in 1938, liked to trace back his Afro-American and Native American ancestors.

Proud Legacy

In the early centuries of their life in the Americas, Black Indians often created a society that might have been a model for everyone. They demonstrated that there was another path through the wilderness than the one hacked out by a European lust for gold, land, and power. Their communities proved bigotry did not rise naturally from American soil, its plains and waters. Bigotry and the appetite for it were imported. They traveled the stormy Atlantic and were speedily transplanted and nourished by those who carried them over.

If they had been of a mind to, Europeans might have learned something from the dark people they selfishly used. Instead, they gathered these peoples' precious gifts and offered promises in return. Africans and Indians followed a tradition that rarely wrote matters down, but held to verbal promises. They met Europeans who wrote many, many things down but failed to keep to their promises or treaties.

What followed in the New World was a titanic European battle for the control of dark people and natural resources. Europe marched out its best soldiers to secure a continent and subdue its people. The result was unending conquest and agonizing slavery.

But beyond the pain were armed Black Indian communities named "Hide Me" and "The Woods Lament For Me." They were home for some of our earliest explorers and pioneers. Families brought up their young, constructed homes, planted and harvested crops, took care of their elderly. They traded with neighbors, instituted religion, government, justice, and planned the common defense.

These settlements not only provided women with an equality and respect unheard of in European society, but elevated some to leadership. Two colonial Brazilian Black Indian communities were commanded by African women, and another African maroon settlement in 1826 in Brazil was ruled by a black woman named Zeferina who successfully led her forces against towns and plantations in Bahia.

With few weapons these alliances in the woods challenged the footholds Europeans built in the Western Hemisphere. Using guerrilla tactics that would become famous in China and Vietnam in our own century, red and black people defeated superior numbers and better equipped foreign armies. This they managed while moving their families out of harm's way. These dark liberators often proved that European rule in the Americas amounted to a thin coat of white paint over a seething dark empire.

Before Patrick Henry shouted "Give me liberty or give me death!" Black Indian maroons acted on this notion. Before Thomas Jefferson wrote "all men are created equal," Black Indians turned a stirring phrase into hard reality. Before the Declaration of Independence eloquently argued for a peoples' revolution against unjust authority, thousands of dark-skinned Americans had been fighting tyrants and slave-hunters on two continents.

For their audacity Black Indians faced a repression more ruthlessly cruel than any King George III imposed on the thirteen original colonies. They were forced to carry on the longest, bloodiest battle for freedom in the Western Hemisphere. Repeatedly they persuaded Europeans it was wiser to grant them independence, sovereignty, and liberty than to continue wars. European powers often learned this lesson late, after they had wasted lives and fortunes on the idea that these free colonies could be easily destroyed.

Maroon wars outlasted the endless conflicts between rival European states. Neither side gave nor asked any quarter, and prisoners were few. For their part maroons, even when captured and facing a terrible death, tried to protect their villagers. More than a century ago a British report from Belem, Brazil, described how a "captured negro gave such an account of the difficulties and dangers of the journey to his settlement, that thirty-three out of the forty [enemy] soldiers refused to accompany their captain."

To prevent Africans and Native Americans from uniting, Europeans played skillfully on racial differences and ethnic rivalries. They kept the pot of animosity boiling. Whites turned Indians into slavehunters and slaveowners, and Africans into "Indian-fighters." Light-skinned Africans were pitted against dark-skinned, free against enslaved, Black Indians against "pure" Africans or "pure" Indians.

Those who have put history into books have emphasized

differences between Africans and Native Americans. For example, they have stressed that Europeans encountered Indians as distinct individuals and members of proud nations, and Africans as nameless slaves. Little mention is made of the enslavement of Native Americans and nothing is said about the cultural similarities between the two dark peoples. In 1984, scholar Theda Perdue said: "By emphasizing the actual, exaggerated and imagined differences between Africans and Indians, whites successfully masked the cultural similarities of the two races as well as their mutual exploitation by whites."

In the United States, Africans became central in the exploration of the new nation, and the development of the crucial fur trade. Because they were more likely to build a binding trust among Native Americans, whites employed them as negotiators and they did not disappoint. Africans, like Native Americans, cherished their own trustworthiness and saw promises and treaties as bonds never to be broken.

In the nineteenth century a Black-Indian friendship limped on despite onslaughts from white racial policies destructive to both peoples. It survives still in the legends of Native American nations, and in the stories and faces of many dark people.

Frontier Myth and Reality

Generations of young minds have been trained to think of life on the American frontier as a saga of white gallantry. Daring pioneers probed the wilderness. John Wayne cowboys whipped Indians to give us the U.S.A. Children of every race rejoiced in this version of the frontier served up each Saturday afternoon at the movies.

In the real wilderness two dark people met and often united. They were not driven together by any special affinity based on a similar skin color. Their meetings were unwittingly arranged by their enemies, the Europeans, who exploited both.

But in the retelling of our western history, no one learned that Africans and Native Americans, separately and to-

*Ben Pickett was born to a Black Cherokee Oklahoma family long
before Oklahoma became a state.*

gether, fought bravely for an America they knew was also theirs. Perhaps their story was trampled underfoot by their hard-riding European foes.

In 1774 patriot James Madison wrote about a slave revolt: "It is prudent such attempts should be concealed as well as suppressed." The Black Indian story has been treated as though it were a massive slave rebellion. Its final burial came at the hands of a later white generation who shaped a heritage for books and movies that ended all claims but white ones.

These frontier omissions lie at the heart of our cherished national myth. The tale of the wilderness stands as the greatest American story ever told. It is the way we wish to see ourselves. "A frontier people," said President Woodrow Wilson, "is, so far, the central and determining fact of our national history. . . . The West is the great word of our history. The Westerner has been the type and master of our American life." Creators of this west did not want it sullied by a black presence or subject to Indian claims.

"The Frontier" went from gritty reality to uplifting truth and finally to national legend. In the process entire races disappeared from it. Its cast of heroic characters included only whites. If Europeans bravely conquered continents, it was not necessary or desirable to show black and red people defying white authority to build their own communities in the wilderness. Racial stereotypes long pictured non-whites as cowardly or childlike. How could red or black men be shown creating a culture in the wilderness, bravely rescuing their families, and riding off into the sunset?

There is another problem in introducing a set of dark frontier heroes. Their love of liberty thrust them against some sainted U.S. figures. Thomas Jefferson, speaking of Indians, said "We would never stop pursuing them with war while one remained on the face of the earth." Andrew Jackson, the first great democrat to reach the White House, was first in a long line of candidates to win the presidency boasting of his Indian-fighting skills. He waged a cruel war against Indian men, women, and children. He staunchly defended slavery and, like Jefferson, owned slaves. To save

These Native American ballplayers, shown at a Dallas, Texas, fair just before World War I, illustrate the blending of Africans and Indians.

their families, Black Indians had to fight off posses and armies launched by these national heroes.

Distorting racial history, as teachers know, injures dark children. They live with a muted heritage. Despite Black Indian contributions to this land, neither black nor Indian children nor their parents have an awareness of this legacy. Like whites, Native Americans learned in school that Africans were contented slaves and had no fighting traditions, certainly none that allied them with Indians. For their part, Afro-Americans are aware of Indians in their family trees. But they probably assume that, like the whites lurking there, they are mere intruders. Such inaccurate beliefs hide a heritage worth exploring. Further, they divide people today who could benefit from unity.

When Black Americans have pursued their genealogy,

This Navajo hunting party, photographed by G.B. Wittick in the 1880s in front of their reservation trading post, demonstrate the U.S. mixture of two dark races.

they have focused on their African roots and sought a meaningful black heritage. Children of the black awareness of the 1960s have rarely cared to mention an Indian ancestry because this might be seen as a denial of their African origins and the value of blackness. All this is part of the racial nightmare we have inherited.

With her usual perception, precision, and pride, Rosa Fay, a Black Seminole living in Brackettville, Texas, in 1943, clarified her peoples' background for pioneer researcher Kenneth W. Porter:

"We's culled people. I don't say we don't has no Injun blood, 'cause we has. But we ain't no Injuns. We's culled people."

Other Americans would benefit from a reexamination of their family trees and a new look at their biological inheritance. The process may yield wonder and gratification where once grief or skepticism ruled.

The ancestors of Black Indians often created—or died in the attempt—an American sisterhood and brotherhood we have tried to attain. They did this under terrible circumstances and in the face of armed opposition.

Had we paid proper attention to their unique model of friendship and loyalty, our common American history, from Hudson Bay to Cape Horn, might have been different, more peaceful. Our racial problems might have been more easily solved. Even at this late date we owe ourselves a rereading of this fascinating legacy. Perhaps we can still learn from and act on its lessons.

2

THEY FLED
AMONGST
THE INDIANS

On July 13, 1984, the people of Roanoke Island, North Carolina, their names emblazoned on books, T-shirts, and silver commemorative medallions, began a year-long celebration. It is their proud claim that U.S. history began with a British settlement on their island. Cultural events throughout the state announced "America's 400th Anniversary," and the U.S. government issued a special "Roanoke Voyages" stamp.

As citizens of a relatively new nation with a short history, we leap at famous firsts and revel in antique events. People feel that our earliest ventures, properly studied, can reveal motives and character in pure form. A study of a first colony on these shores could yield insights into the nature of colonization and cast light on how and why this nation developed. Our schools spend much time studying our earliest European colonies. Teachers use this focus to teach children simple object lessons in their white ancestors' flinty determination to survive and prevail.

If the children are of African or Native American descent, they learn that their ancestors lost badly and ingloriously, but that was all for the best anyway. The historical record often does not agree with these kinds of conclusions. The English newcomers sent to Roanoke Island in 1584 by Sir Walter Raleigh are a case in point. What these pioneers did was self-destruct over their own love of possession. When a silver cup allegedly disappeared, the Roanoke men roared out of their tiny enclave, muskets and torches in hand, to destroy their Indian neighbors' village and crops. This blazing display of European possession-mania cut the colony off from the one local source of help.

When the Spanish Armada severed the settlement's connection to British ports, it withered and died. Roanoke Island became famous as "the lost colony."

In light of this unacceptable object lesson for children, most school texts prefer to begin U.S. history with another colony, Captain John Smith's Jamestown, Virginia, founded in 1607. Captain Smith was sent out by a London joint-stock company seeking profits from colonization. Smith sailed with an overload of failed aristocrats and settled on land owned by the Algonquin Confederacy.

Trouble began when the newcomers refused to plant, build, or exert themselves. Iron revolver in hand, Captain Smith ordered his lazy gentlemen to "work or starve." Time and again the English were rescued from starvation through the generosity of the Algonquin Confederacy, which provided corn and bread. The foreigners responded by refusing to share their European agricultural tools with the Indians and violence soon broke out.

At Roanoke Island colonization proved a total failure. At Jamestown, what collapsed was the European "work ethic." No wonder some historians decided that U.S. history did not begin until the arrival of the hard-working Pilgrims aboard the *Mayflower* in 1620. Leaping over events can avoid some unpleasant conclusions about early European motives, character, and success.

The First Foreign Colony on U.S. Soil

If the first foreign colony on U.S. land is worthy of study, then another contender for this title also deserves consideration. Less than two generations after Columbus first landed in 1492, and while his son Diego served as governor of Hispaniola, a Spanish-controlled island in the Caribbean, a colony was started on the mainland of South Carolina. No one seems to want to celebrate or even mention its dramatic story and this is unfortunate. It offers a feast of insights into some errors that still cast their shadow on our racial problems.

In June 1526, Lucas Vásquez de Ayllón, a wealthy Spanish official in the city of Santo Domingo on Hispaniola, founded a colony at or near the mouth of the Pee Dee River in eastern South Carolina. Six decades before Roanoke Island, eight decades before Jamestown, and almost a century before the *Mayflower* landed at Plymouth Rock, Ayllón began his North American dream.

Ayllón's effort has been overlooked, perhaps because most people prefer to believe that U.S. life began with the arrival of English-speaking Anglo-Saxons living under British law. Perhaps his settlement is neglected because of its tragic fate—death by mismanagement, disease, and slave revolt. Perhaps it is unmentioned because of its unique rebirth in the woods by people not considered a part of the white U.S. heritage.

Ayllón began preparing for his great adventure in 1520 by sending Captain Francisco Gordillo to locate a good landing site and build friendly relations with the local inhabitants. Instead, the captain teamed up with a slave-hunter, Pedro de Quexos. While failing to survey a site or build good relations with anyone, the two men captured seventy Native Americans and brought them back to Santo Domingo as slaves. The first European act on what is now U.S. soil was that of making slaves of free men and women.

The two adventurers returned to Ayllón with stories of naming a great river in honor of St. John the Baptist and having cut Christian crosses in trees. Ayllón was not impressed with their seizure of seventy Native Americans and brought the issue to the attention of a commission presided over by Diego Columbus. The Indians were declared free and ordered returned, but Spanish records do not show whether the order was carried out.

But they do show that Ayllón, to make amends with the natives who lost their loved ones, sent the slaver Quexos who started the problem. Once again Quexos returned with other captured natives he claimed had volunteered to serve as guides for the Spanish expedition.

Meanwhile Ayllón retained one of the original seventy, Ferdinand Chicorana, as his New World interpreter. Impressed with his skills and understanding of the mainland, he brought Chicorana to Spain to meet the king. After this meeting the king issued an order permitting Ayllón to sail for the coast of North America. The king's orders forbade enslavement of the Indians, and added "you be very careful about the treatment of the Indians." Three Dominican missionaries were sent along to protect Native Americans from the Europeans.

With this record as a backdrop, Ayllón prepared to launch his expedition to North America. After some delays his fleet of six vessels sailed from Puerto de la Plata. Aboard were five hundred Spanish men and women, one hundred enslaved Africans, six or seven dozen horses, and physicians, sailors, and the Dominican priests.

Mishap and disaster dogged the enterprise as it landed on the wrong coast, lost a ship, and Chicorana deserted. The other native interpreters seized by Quexos also fled. The Europeans were on their own.

Determined to succeed, Ayllón drove his people until they came to a great river, which was probably the Pee Dee. Selecting a location in a low, marshy area, Ayllón ordered his band to set up camp. He paused to name his settlement "San Miguel de Gualdape." When he ordered the Africans to begin building homes, he launched black slavery in the United States.

The neighboring natives fled inland and kept away. It was probably enough for them that the same Europeans who

had seized seventy of their loved ones had now returned
with Africans in chains.

Europeans, arriving to exploit land and labor, contrasted
in many ways with the peaceful natives. The Indians lived
harmoniously with nature and shared huge pine, weather-
insulated homes that slept about three hundred people each.
Europeans tried to construct homes that kept men and
women in separate rooms. Europeans wrote that these Indians lived long lives and "their old age is robust." While
European men dominated their women, Indian women doc-
tors served their people plant juices to cure fevers.

While native life moved peacefully ahead, the foreigners
slipped toward disaster. Disease and starvation ravaged their
colony and internal disputes tore it apart. The river was full
of fish, but few Europeans were well enough to fish. Then
an epidemic swept the settlement and before housing was in
place wintery winds blew in.

Ayllón became gravely ill and died on October 18, after
having named his nephew, Johan Ramirez his successor.
But Ramirez was in Puerto Rico, and the leaderless Spaniards split into bitter armed factions. Men drew swords and
marched in howling winds to arrest and sometimes execute
those who would become leaders of the colony. Some survivors complained that in the midst of their tribulations
Africans began setting fires, and Native Americans sided
with the slaves and made trouble.

In November a crisis erupted when Africans rebelled and
fled to the Indians. One authority on slave revolts believes
this was instigated by Native Americans angry over whites
using their land. Africans, used to freedom in their homeland, probably needed no prodding from outside to strike
for liberty. They understandably fled a dying European
colony and slavery, and saw an opportunity to begin new
lives in the woods among people who also hated slavery.

The surviving 150 Spanish men and women, no longer
able to face a freezing winter without shelter or their labor
supply, packed up and left for Santo Domingo. It would be
another quarter of a century before Spaniards would again
build a North American colony with slave labor.

San Miguel de Gualdape was not a total failure as the first foreign colony on U.S. soil. The Europeans left for home after five months, but Africans remained to build their own society with the Native Americans. In the unplanned way that history meanders and careens, a new community emerged in the woods, which also included foreigners from overseas, the Africans. This new mixed settlement would soon have many American models.

In distant South Carolina forests, two and a half centuries before the Declaration of Independence, two dark peoples first lit the fires of freedom and exalted its principles. Though neither white, Christian, nor European, they became the first settlement of any permanence on these shores to include people from overseas. As such, they qualify as our earliest inheritance.

There is no way of knowing how long the settlement remained free of European intervention. Within a century the march of white conquest would spill into their lovely streams and forests. But while this Black Indian community lived, it provided the Americas with an example of frontier hospitality and democratic camaraderie.

Some among us will mourn the symbolic loss of the white pioneers of Roanoke Island, Jamestown, or Plymouth. The fables about them make pleasant reading. But their supporters can take heart from the brave heritage bequeathed us by the dark freedom-fighters who fled San Miguel de Gualdape and by the Native Americans who took them in as sisters and brothers. Here is a gallant American tradition that ranks with those established by other fighting Americans at Concord Bridge and Valley Forge.

The story of this new community shows that our vaunted democracy did not march into the wilderness with buckled shoes and British accents. Rather it was dancing around fireplaces in South Carolina wrapped in dried animal skins and singing African and native songs before the British arrived. This dark democracy lived in family groups before London companies sent out settlers with muskets, Bibles, and concepts of private property.

The Black Indians of the Pee Dee River became the first

colony on this continent to practice the belief that all people
—newcomer and native—are created equal and are entitled
to life, liberty, and the pursuit of happiness. Theirs is a
story worth remembering and worth teaching our children.

It Began with Columbus

For the people of the Americas the arrival of Columbus was
hardly a blessing. On his first day, October 12, 1492, the
explorer wrote in his Diary "I took some of the natives by
force." He later found the original inhabitants to be "trac-
table," "peaceable," and concluded "there is not in the world
a better nation." His response as a European was to say that
Indians must be "made to work . . . and adopt our ways."

The Christopher Columbus whose unique seamanship
and courage had opened the Americas to European penetra-
tion also began the transatlantic slave trade. He started by
shipping ten chained Arawak men and women to Seville,
Spain. He wrote enthusiastically to King Ferdinand and
Queen Isabella about the business possibilities: "From here,
in the name of the Blessed Trinity, we can send all the slaves
that can be sold." When he loaded 1100 Taino men and
women aboard four Spanish ships, the crowding and the
stormy Atlantic crossing took a fearful toll. Only three
hundred survived. But Columbus and Spain had decided to
continue the profitable slave trade from the Americas.
Seville became the slave capital of Spain.

Spanish priests were the first to denounce the horrors of
bondage. In 1511 Dominican Friar Montesinos called slavery a mortal sin and said cruelty and tyrannny over Indians
could not be justified by Christians. A few years later Bishop
Las Casas, who had witnessed countless Indian massacres
by his fellow Spaniards, blamed greed for the horrors: "They
kill them [Indians] because they want to be rich and have
much gold, which is their sole aim." Las Casas concluded
that in the New World Spaniards had become devils and
Indians were the only true Christians.

Las Casas led a determined effort to halt Indian bondage.
He pointed out that Indians died off by the thousands from

This photograph taken at the Shiprock Indian Agency during the early part of this century shows a mixture of people common in the southwest since the 1500s—European priest, Native Americans, and Afro-Americans.

slavery and European diseases. Forced labor in Spanish mines in the Americas was so harsh that the average worker died before he was twenty-six.

To meet their need for more laborers, Europeans looked next to Africa. The strongest sons and daughters of Africa were seized in their homes or fields or purchased from local traders. They were packed into cargo ships and shipped across the Atlantic. Thomas Branagan, a Dublin youth who for many years served as a seaman aboard slave ships, described the boarding scene:

> Children are torn from their distracted parents; parents from their screaming children; wives from their frantic husbands; husbands from their violated wives; brothers from their loving sisters; sisters from their affectionate brothers. See them collected in flocks, and like a herd of swine, driven to the ships. They cry, they struggle, they resist; but all in vain. No eye pities, no hand helps.

The first Africans brought to the New World by European slavers probably arrived in April 1502 aboard the ship that brought the new governor of Hispaniola, Nicolas de Ovando. Soon after they landed, some Africans escaped to the woods and found a new home among the Native Americans. Later that year Governor Ovando sent a request to King Ferdinand that no more Africans be sent to the Americas. His reason was simple: "They fled amongst the Indians and taught them bad customs, and never could be captured."

Why did he feel they could never be retaken? Had the two peoples united as a military force at this early date? Were Native Americans prepared to drive off European slavehunters? Was an alliance taking shape in the woods between two peoples who opposed the Spanish conquerors? The answers to these questions are unclear.

But Governor Ovando is describing more than a problem of bad, untrustworthy servants. His words are more than a complaint about the difficulties of recapturing fugitives in a tropical rainforest. Governor Ovando's words in 1502 are the first hint of a growing problem for the European masters of the New World, the first notice of a new relationship budding beyond the control of the Spaniards.

Africans arrived on these shores with valuable assets for both Europeans and Native Americans. They were used to agricultural labor and working in field gangs, something unfamiliar to most Indians. As experts in tropical agriculture, they had a lot to teach both white and red people. Further, Africans had a virtual immunity to European diseases such as smallpox, which wiped out Native Americans.

For Europeans seeking a source of labor that could not escape, Africans were ideal because they were three thousand miles from home. They could not flee to loved ones, as Indian slaves could. The African man and woman who fled could always be identified by skin color, and black became the badge of bondage.

Native Americans soon discovered that Africans had some gifts that made them uniquely valuable. Through their slave experience they qualified as experts on whites—their diplomacy, armaments, motives, strengths, and weaknesses.

Escaped slaves came bearing a knowledge of their masters' languages, defenses, and plans. Sometimes Africans were able to carry off muskets, machetes, or valuable gunpowder. For these reasons their role could be crucial to Native Americans, their place secure in village life. A common foe, not any special affinity of skin color, became the first link of friendship, the earliest motivation for alliance.

Next the two peoples began to discover they shared some vital views of life. Family was of basic importance to both, with children and the elderly treasured. Religion was a daily part of cultural life, not merely practiced on Sundays. Both Africans and Native Americans found they shared a belief in economic cooperation rather than competition and rivalry. Each race was proud, but neither was weighed down by prejudice. Skill, friendship, and trust, not skin color or race were important. Since Indians willingly adopted people into their villages, Africans found they were welcome.

In the century following Columbus's landing, millions of Native Americans died from a combination of European diseases, harsh treatment, and murder. Africans took their places in the mines and fields of the New World. The 80 million Native Americans alive in 1492 became only 10 million left alive a century later. But the 10,000 Africans working in the Americas in 1527, had by the end of the century become 90,000 people.

These figures are even more striking within local areas. In 1519 when the Spaniards arrived, Mexico had a population of 25 million Indians. By the end of the century only a million were still alive. The invader calculated that more profit would be made if laborers were worked to death and replaced. In their plans pain and suffering did not count, and no cruelty was considered excessive.

Out of the shifting labor forces a new population emerged of mixed Africans and Native Americans. By 1650 Mexico alone had an African-Indian population (some with white ancestry) of one hundred thousand. A new race was being born.

In 1510 King Ferdinand, visions of gold dancing before his eyes, lifted all restrictions on sending Africans to the

Opposite page:
Often with clerical blessings and prayers for last minute conversions,
Native American royalty was burned at the stake. The Inca of Peru is
ceremonially put to death by explorer Pizarro and his armed forces.

These Black Indians of southern Mexico used such primitive
weapons as the bow and arrow to protect their families from modern
European weaponry.

Americas. He promised to send all that were needed and include "a trustworthy person" to be in charge of each group. In this way, he said, slaves and masters would "share in the gold they may collect" and slaves would receive "ease if they work well." This was an idle dream.

The slave population expanded, but was never rewarded with ease for its great toil. European masters continued to drive those in chains as hard as they could. Ease only came when people escaped to the forests and swamps. Increasingly Africans and the remaining enslaved Indians fled their masters and created their own secret colonies beyond European eyes. In time these would pose the most disruptive challenge the European economic system in colonial America ever faced.

In the age of Columbus and Las Casas this threat was not clear. Europeans counted their profits and kept importing Africans. In 1511 Governor Ovando forgot his opposition to importing Africans as slaves. "One black," he marveled, "can do the work of four Indians." Here, he believed, was a danger worth the price. His fellow Europeans heartily agreed with him. From then on slavery would expand, brutality would keep it in place, and whites would reap enormous profits.

3

BETWEEN THE RACES WE CANNOT DIG TOO DEEP A GULF

In 1522 Europeans in the Americas first learned that slavery did not easily lead to enormous wealth. On Christmas Day, African and Indian slaves on a plantation owned by Diego Columbus rose and murdered their masters and overseers. Nearby Native Americans joined the rebels. The beautiful island of Hispaniola shook with the first recorded slave rebellion in the New World.

The conspiracy had spread across the sprawling sugar plantations in the weeks before Christmas. Patiently the plotters waited until Christmas Day when the planters and their families would be bloated with food, soaked with liquor, and too weak or sleepy to offer much resistance. Then they struck, plunging into the night to kill whites and find freedom.

For two days they met little opposition, but on the third Spanish troops caught up with the rebels in an open field

33

and opened fire. The fugitives broke for the woods. The Europeans were unfamiliar with the treacherous terrain near the city of Santo Domingo. Few were willing to pursue their most dangerous slaves into an area suited to guerrilla warfare.

Governor Diego Columbus, his Spanish troops and advisors, decided on a new strategy. The governor hired Native Americans for the dangerous task of tracking the fugitives. A hunt began. The exact outcome is unclear.

Slavery and Resistance Spread

Masters and slaves learned some important lessons from this first bloody confrontation. Enslaving Indians and Africans was not going to be free of pain. Masters in a slave land would not sleep easily each night. Europeans concluded it was absolutely necessary to remain armed, and use one race to fight the other. A French colonial dispatch later in the century put the matter simply: "The law is hard, but it is both wise and necessary in a land of 15 slaves to one white. Between the races we cannot dig too deep a gulf."

The enslaved also learned some lessons. Their owners would rise to any level of violence and arm anyone to protect bondage and their grip on the Americas. Europeans would throw their own soldiers into the fray or hire Indians living nearby. Slaves began to reason that their success might depend upon their ability to make friends among neighboring Indians. Friends do not hunt friends.

The European policy of divide and conquer that began on Christmas Day, 1522, introduced elements of deep division to the Americas. Slavery and its cruel legacy left a bloody trail across the grass and soil of the Americas. It spread southward and westward from the Caribbean to Mexico and along the coastline of South America to Cape Horn where Atlantic and Pacific oceans meet.

But another American tradition also took root. The men and women enslaved in the New World began a pattern of resistance. The first enslaved were the first to flee, the first to rebel, the first to announce that chains were meant to be broken.

Colonial armies searched the rivers, forests, and fields for maroons and their organized colonies.

The spirit of rebellion spread like a wildfire that no European power could put out. In the next ten years revolts spread to Colombia, Panama, Cuba, Puerto Rico, and Mexico. In 1537 a major insurrection threatened Spanish headquarters at Mexico City. Viceroy Antonio de Mendoza reported that Africans "had chosen a King, and had agreed . . . to kill all the Spaniards . . . and that the Indians were also with them." Terrified Mexican officials agreed to halt any further importations of Africans. Slave resistance had temporarily halted the African slave trade.

By the 1570s the flames of revolt were burning brightly in Mexico. One in every ten slaves was living a free life in hiding. Alarmed about the safety of whites, Viceroy Martin Enriquez (1568–1580) wrote to the king of Spain:

Your Majesty, . . . the time is coming when these [African]
people will have become masters of the Indians, inasmuch
as they were born among them and their maidens, and are
men who dare to die as well as any Spaniard in the world.
. . . I do not know who will be in a position to resist
them.

It was in Mexico that Europeans made their strongest
effort to keep Africans apart from Native Americans. Black
men far outnumbered their women and so sought Indian
wives. A Native American wife meant, if she was free, that
children born to her would be free, not slaves. So extensive

*This old French engraving of the Osage Indian Nation shows the
variation in color types present in one Native American Nation.
(Note how all faces have been "romanized" with straight noses.)*

was the contact between red and black people that Spanish law prohibited the two races from living together or marrying. As early as 1523, Hernando Cortés was given a Royal Order to keep Indians in their villages, apart from Africans at all costs. (This was only seven years after Venice, Italy, isolated its Jews in the first ghetto in history.)

One Royal Order forbade "trade, commerce or communication" between the two dark peoples. They were forbidden to sell chickens, fruit, and vegetables, and both defied the law.

Racial mixing was so common in Mexico that it became hard to tell by skin color who was free and who was slave. King Philip complained that young Black Indians committed crimes and then dressed as Indians so they could "hide out with their mother's relatives and cannot be found." The genetic blending of the two peoples clearly weakened the control Europeans wanted over their slaves. Europeans feared any dark person might be a slave driven to desperation or out for revenge. "One lived in constant fear," wrote a Spanish colonist.

Maroon Settlements

From the time of Columbus the gravest threat to European domination of the Western Hemisphere came from outlaw communities of former slaves. These maroon colonies, as they were called, were considered a knife poised at the throat of the slave system. Some fearful Europeans saw them as a sword pressed against the entire colonial system in the Americas.

Men and women who lived in them saw their settlements as the fulfillment of an American dream—a sheltered home in freedom. They were a place for families to educate their young, develop their agriculture and trade, practice religion, justice, and government. As outlaw communities they operated in remote, difficult-to-find and hard-to-defeat locations. Maroons considered each day of survival a small miracle, and were thankful for each new dawn as free men and women.

Entitled "America," this antique French engraving shows African and Native American people living in harmony and happiness in their own village.

Some colonies were begun by a single African or Indian, and others were the result of several or many slaves fleeing together. The history of the Saramaka people of Surinam in South America started around 1685 when African and native slaves escaped and together formed a maroon society. For eight generations Dutch armed forces tried to crush their community, but today it is still alive and boasts twenty thousand members. For the Saramakans liberty came in 1761 when Europeans abandoned their wars and sued for peace.

From their first day maroon colonies faced enormous problems. They had to quickly find a safe location, plan a defense, feed and clothe their people, and plan the life of a stable community. Women were usually in short supply, and many maroon raids sought to bring back African or Indian wives. Families meant that communities would last, remain at peace, and that their soldiers would fight harder because their loved ones and children were at risk.

Some maroons perched near large cities and lived as bandits. They raided local plantations, merchants, and even Indians and slaves. Their communities were unstable, often had few women and no children, and usually disappeared into the violence they helped create. Although some earned a reputation for daring raids on rich Europeans, most were feared by people of every race.

Fear of attack haunted every maroon settlement. It was a danger they could count on. Johannes King, an African who lived among the Matawai Indians in the Guianas in 1885, recalled his peoples' struggle to stay alive during decades of warfare.

Here is the story of our ancestors and of their difficulties while they were at war with the bakra [whites]. At that time they suffered severe shortages and were living under dreadful conditions, but the lack of food was their worst problem. They didn't even have time to clear and plant gardens to produce food. The whites were always pursuing and attacking. . . . They slashed the crops to bits, ruining everything they saw. They set fire to everything they didn't want to carry off with them. Well, that enraged our early ancestors against the whites.

The planning of defense and agriculture in most Black Indian settlements drew largely on African models and experience. However, no type of influence was discarded, and these colonies grasped aspects of Indian, African, and even slave life considered vital for survival.

The African influence was strongest in tropical maroon locations, and there African methods of planting, irrigation, and harvesting held sway under African-type governments. Africans, as experts on tropical agriculture, had a lot to teach both Indians and Europeans. A leading defense technique—planting sharp sticks in a pit and covering it with thick grass to trap intruding armies—was African. It not only inflicted terrible damage, but terrified any invading army with the thought that a sudden, painful death could occur at any moment. These pits were almost impossible to detect.

Men and women, who once were starved and beaten by masters, grew strong and vigorous in these hidden communities. Maroon settlements took such daring names as: God Knows Me and None Else, Disturb Me If You Dare, Come Try Me If You Be Men, and I Shall Moulder Before I Shall Be Taken.

Maroon self-esteem seemed to grow with each month of liberty. It also sprang from the knowledge that Europeans were often afraid to march out and challenge their communities' defenses. "Their self-respect grows because of the fear whites have of them," wrote a Portuguese colonist to King João in 1719.

Maroon music also reflected the confidence settlements had in their military strength. A maroon song, preserved for generations in Brazil, assured villagers their enemies were doomed:

Black man rejoice
  White man won't come here
And if he does,
  The Devil will take him off.

Maroon culture drew from the experiences of Africa's nations, Native Americans, and what each of these peoples learned about Europeans as slaves or free men and women. Africans, so far from home, made special efforts to preserve their ancestral ways and pass them on to their children and others who would listen. African patterns, prominent in farming and defense, were also important in government, administration of justice, and religion.

Many maroon colonies adopted forms of Christianity, but allowed a number of competing religions to flourish. In some villages and families mystic religions played a vital part in the way people faced the terrible threats around

This old French engraving shows maroon leaders being condemned to death for leading rebellions against European authorities.

them. Maroons were convinced that each day still alive was worthy of a blessing to a powerful outside force.

To the surprise of Europeans, many maroon colonies became successful, independent farming communities. In the eighteenth century Captain John Stedman, leading Dutch troops against maroons in the Guianas, wrote that maroon foods were superior to European products and in great supply. Men and women in maroon settlements were often described as healthy, tall, and muscular, a tribute to their diets and to their freedom.

For some colonies trade became a vital part of economic life. Men and women ventured out to exchange their farm produce for valuable guns and ammunition, and sometimes gold and jewelry. Trade was carried on with slaves and masters, Indians and Europeans, and free black people.

The prosperity of some colonies made them an object of envy and then attack by Europeans. Those maroons most

likely to face military assaults by invading armies were
situated on land Europeans wanted. Others were invaded
because they were engaged in businesses whites sought to
control.

Black Indians in Venezuela in 1728, for example, ran a
successful shipping operation Europeans wanted. Led by a
man named Juan Andresote, they carried cacao from Spanish merchants in the Yaracuy valley to Dutch merchants on
Curaçao about 150 miles away. Philip V of Spain awarded
his European friends a monopoly of this trade, placing them
on a collision course with the business run by Andresote. In
1732 Spain sent out 250 soldiers, including 150 men conscripted from Indians and African slaves, to challenge the
dark businessmen of Andresote.

Outside the town of Cabria, Andresote quickly changed
from shipping expert to guerrilla warrior. He maneuvered
his army into battle with such skill that the slave and native
soldiers deserted the European command. Andresote's
sharpshooters' musket fire then brought down all but forty-
four European soldiers.

But Spain had not given up. It sent 1500 troops after
Andresote, and he had to slip off to Curaçao to save his life.
His brother, José Francisco, rallied the Black Indians, but
they were no match for such an overwhelming force. However, it did take Spain another five years to eliminate their
dark business competitors in the Yaracuy valley.

It is hard to tell whether Europeans more often fought or
traded with their Black Indian competitors. Colonial law
often threw whites into jail for trading with the outlawed
maroon communities on their borders. But some Europeans
considered this a cost to be borne in carrying on a successful
business. It may have seemed strange to have former slaves
and their former masters trading like equals, but both saw
a profit in the exchange and conducted themselves like good
business people.

Maroon Governments and Leaders

Maroon settlements were an effort to re-create a free society by people who had once lived free. Before 1700 most maroon leaders were—like their followers—African-born. Some of these colonies built dynasties on African models that lasted for generations and had royal courts, cabinets, princes, and princesses.

By the beginning of the eighteenth century maroon figures were cut from a different mold. They were born in the Americas, often of Black Indian stock. Their skills were in dealing with Europeans in battle and at the negotiating table. They preferred to be known as governor or commander rather than king or queen. Most leaders still had a familiarity with African traditions and customs.

Women played a crucial role in maroon life and were considered for leadership. Filippa Maria Aranha, an African, ruled a thriving colony in Amazonia, Brazil. Her daring forays against the Portuguese armies sent against her village not only defeated them, but convinced the enemy it was wiser to negotiate than try to defeat her. At the bargaining table Aranha won her people's liberty and sovereignty. In Passanha, Brazil, the Portuguese discovered Malali Indians and Africans living under the rule of another African woman.

Leading a maroon colony took a rare combination of wisdom, toughness, and skill. The ruler had to provide for a strong defense, keep spirits high despite all threats, and develop a rich and satisfying economic life for members. Courts or other means of administering justice had to be in place and considered fair. Because of the threat from outside, enforcement of rules was often harsh and swift. On vital matters such as murder, robbery, adultery, or desertion, the punishment was death, often in public.

Since women were outnumbered by men in maroon settlements, women were not only protected, but sometimes permitted to have more than one husband. This arrangement was carried out under careful rules that kept jealousy from disrupting village life. In this as in all other matters

This engraving of a maroon warrior by a Dutch artist captures his steadfast determination to resist European efforts to end the freedom of his family and friends.

preserving unity and providing a strong defense came first. These settlements also protected the young and the elderly with special care, since the former represented the future and the latter represented gallant traditions and valuable knowledge.

Maroon leaders were first and foremost military figures. For over four centuries in Latin America European armed forces waged a war to the death against them.

Captain John Stedman, a British officer in charge of Dutch troops in Guiana at the time of the American Revolution, left a complete record of his maroon campaigns. He told how his troops, which included Europeans and Indians, destroyed "the most beautiful field of ripe rice" and left a village of one hundred homes "in smoking ruins." Captain

Stedman, his eighty marines and twenty rangers, enjoyed their devastation, and he proudly wrote of "the continued noise of the firing, shouting and swearing, and hallooing of black and white men mixed together; the groans of the wounded and dying, all weltering in blood and dust."

To delay or defeat these well-armed soldiers, maroons had to devise careful strategies. In one battle Stedman's men all suffered wounds from maroon musket fire, but realized they had only minor injuries. Instead of bullets embedded in their flesh, they found pebbles, coat buttons, and pieces of silver coins. These maroons had no bullets.

On the night after the battle, Stedman's troops found themselves in the midst of a shouting match with their maroon foes. All night voices from the woods hurled curses and ridicule at the invaders, and the Europeans shouted back their fury at being kept awake. The next morning Stedman's soldiers discovered that, under the cover of that noise, the maroons had moved out their women, children, and elderly, their rice, yams, and other possessions. The Captain thought this tactic "would have done honor to any European commander."

By the time Captain Stedman and his soldiers left for Holland in 1776, the maroon forces had grown from three thousand to fifteen thousand. Sixty years later they were seventy thousand strong and enjoying their liberty, prosperity, and independence.

To defeat them, Captain Stedman had relied on conscripted Indian and slave soldiers. This became a common European practice. These troops proved to be the best jungle fighters the Europeans had. They also were the least reliable, the most likely to defect to the dark people they were sent off to destroy. European soldiers and officers rarely relished marching into the wilderness to face seasoned jungle fighters, so they continued to conscript, bribe, or hire Native Americans and Africans.

The Republic of Palmares

For almost a century a maroon colony called the Republic of Palmares, in northeastern Brazil, stood as the greatest challenge to European rule in Latin America. It began around 1600 with a few slave runaways and friendly Indians. In 1640 a Dutch citizen named Lintz reported eleven thousand people living in Palmares's three villages. The Dutch West India Company decided to put Palmares through "fire and sword." They tried again a few years later, also without success.

By then Palmares was half a mile long, with streets six feet wide, and had hundreds of homes, churches, and shops. Its well-kept lands produced cereals and other crops irrigated African-style with streams. It boasted courts that carried out justice for its thousands of citizens, and was ruled over by King Ganga-Zumba. (Ganga-Zumba combined an Angolan African word for *great* with a Tupi Indian word for *ruler*.) Christianity was commonly practiced, including elaborate marriage and baptism ceremonies that drew large crowds.

In 1657 life in Palmares was still relatively peaceful. But the new rulers of Brazil, the Portuguese, decided it must be destroyed. A foreign expedition was launched every fifteen months to obliterate the Republic of Palmares, and each was beaten back with heavy losses on both sides. Palmares, its determined armed forces, and three huge surrounding walls, cost many a foreign commander or governor his post or his life. Men in splendid uniforms turned and fled back to Rio de Janeiro or Lisbon, relieved to abandon a war they could not win.

A seventeenth-century Portuguese soldier wrote of these failures: "The army's best fighters, the most experienced leaders . . . were at once employed for this purpose, with immense effort and suffering, but very little was achieved."

Finally, in 1694, the invaders brought in an army of Brazilian Indians called "Paulistas" to lead the massive assault on the Republic of Palmares. Some six thousand Paulistas, supported by Portuguese soldiers and weapons, laid seige to Palmares for forty-two days. On February 5 it was overrun, with hundreds dying in hand-to-hand combat. Other hundreds, including Palmares's bravest warriors, according to a legend, hurled themselves over a cliff rather than surrender.

The ruler, King Zambi, who had been wounded in the struggle, was captured and beheaded by the enemy. His head was displayed, said the European victors, "to kill the legend of his immortality."

But death does not kill legends. For almost a century the Republic of Palmares had shone as the brightest star of freedom in Latin America. It had united many peoples under an African form of government and culture. For generations it had met and turned around European invaders and their hired mercenaries. Each time it had returned to planting and harvesting abundant crops.

The meaning of Palmares and its legendary rulers was that dark people in the Western Hemisphere meant to be free. This idea terrified Europeans more than the powerful armies and defenses of Palmares.

The President of Mexico

In 1615 King Philip II of Spain received a letter from his Mexican colony advising him that "division of the races is an indispensable element" in controlling his colonies. But dark people had also learned the reverse was true, that their best road to success in resisting foreign domination was to unite. This became clear during the crucial war for independence Mexico fought against Spain early in the nineteenth century.

Not only did Mexico's maroon experience prepare its dark people and mixed races to march to independence, but it cast up a leader in Vincente Guerrero, a Black Indian. Born in Ixtla in 1782, Guerrero's parents were of mixed European, Indian, and African stock. As a young man, Guerrero became a mule driver, and in 1810, he was one of the first to enlist in the war for independence.

In his first battle, he was commissioned a captain. As the

conflict dragged on for years, the leading revolutionaries died or were captured. But with two thousand ragged men carrying guns and ammunition taken from fallen Spanish soldiers, Guerrero kept the spark of rebellion alive in the Sierra Madre mountains. Repeatedly Spanish officials tried to persuade the charismatic young man to surrender and return home. They even sent his father to ask him to accept a pardon. Guerrero fought on.

By 1821 the independence movement was headed toward success. Guerrero's incorruptibility gave it strength and drew peasant support. "His swarthy face, resonant voice, and flashing eyes made him an object of profound respect even among his enemies," reported U.S. historian H. H. Bancroft. In 1824 Guerrero, who had only learned to read a few years before (when he was forty), helped shape the Mexican Constitution. He wrote the provision "All inhabitants whether White, African, or Indian, are qualified to hold office."

In 1829 the former mule driver became President of Mexico. He began a program of far-reaching reforms, abolishing the death penalty, starting construction of schools and libraries for the poor. He ended slavery in Mexico. Yet, because of his skin color, lack of education, and country manner, he was held in contempt by the upper classes in Mexico City.

This president who had, according to Bancroft, "a gentleness and magnetism that inspired love among his adherents," was still "a triple-blooded outsider."

Black historian J. A. Rogers summarized Guerrero's striking accomplishments by calling him "the George Washington and Abraham Lincoln of Mexico."

4

THE FINEST LOOKING PEOPLE I HAVE EVER SEEN

First they came one or two at a time, strong young men and women beating a path from slavery into the thickets and marshes of Florida. Soon others joined them, sisters and brothers, mothers and fathers, then the elderly and the very young. Parents carried babies or children, some injured during escape. Daring men returned to Georgia and Alabama to fetch mothers, fathers, wives, children, and friends who needed help in reaching freedom.

Florida proved unique in U.S. history—a location where large communities of ex-slaves could live hidden from enemy eyes. Escaped slaves living as maroons became Florida's first settlers. Dense jungles, high grass, deadly reptiles, alligators, hordes of insects, and tropical diseases waited for all who entered.

These conditions also protected Africans from European invading forces. Historian Joseph Opala has written:

"Politically, Florida was in the hands of its new inhabitants. That it was colored Spanish on the map was largely for the amusement of white men."

Generations before Thomas Jefferson sat down to write the Declaration of Independence. Florida's dark runaways wrote their own. It used no paper or ink and was constructed of spears, arrows, and captured muskets. But it issued a warning of "keep out!" and "leave us alone, or else die." It said "liberty or death."

Seminoles and Africans

Around the time African settlers arrived in Florida, refugees from the Creek Nation also settled there. This group called themselves "Seminoles" or runaways, and their Muskogee culture accepted a variety of Indian ethnic groups—Yuchi, Hitchiti, and Alabama. For Seminole people used to admitting those who were different, it was easy to accept Africans.

Africans proved far more familiar with Florida's tropical terrain than Spaniards or Seminoles. They transplanted a rice cultivation method practiced in Senegambia and Sierra Leone. Used to a more moderate climate, Seminoles began to learn how to survive in Florida from these ex-slaves. "From the beginning of Seminole colonization in Florida," writes Opala, "the Indian may have depended upon African farmers for their survival."

The Seminole Nation offered their new friends some valuable gifts in return. Africans and other ethnic groups enjoyed an independent village status. Their only obligation was to pay a small agricultural tax to be used for the common defense.

If Africans needed something besides freedom, it was a strong defense against slavehunters from the north, so their tax was well spent. Georgia slaveholders were soon invading Florida, seeking their runaways, and were soon meeting a united resistance by red and black armed forces.

Black Seminoles tried to live a peaceful life in their towns and around their ceremonial plazas ruled by their own

With muskets and ammunition taken from the European invaders, red and black Seminoles fought for their right to live in peace in Florida.

chiefs. While they were shaping a sturdy agricultural community, British officers to the north provided weapons and military advisors for desperadoes ready to raid Florida for slave fugitives.

With hostile British forces closing in on its Florida

border, Spain recruited anyone willing to fight these invaders. Florida became a Spanish buffer zone protected by
Native American and African warriors, assisted by a
sprinkling of pirates, smugglers, and others.

In 1739 slave fugitives living in St. Augustine built a fort
to protect their families and stem British incursions. Spain,
with few of its own soldiers, was pleased to have their
lands protected by these dark men. The English were furious
about a fort guarded by hundreds of armed Africans and
their Indian soul mates.

Black Seminoles played a vital part in the coalition
against the slave power to the north. Their knowledge of
farming in Florida was second to none. They also brought
the kind of information slaves always have about their
masters' ways of thinking. One observer described them as
"stout and even gigantic . . . the finest looking people I
have ever seen." They were almost immune to the malaria
and small pox that devastated Indians and Europeans.

British and then U.S. slaveholders were horrified by the
strong relationships among red and black Seminoles. Each
owed the other a measure of devotion and service, and this
was hardly what whites had come to expect from Africans.
Black Seminoles had well-built homes and raised fine crops
of corn, sweet potatoes, vegetables, and cotton. They owned
herds of livestock and had time for hunting and fishing.
They were known for their excellent fighting skills, a major
in the Georgia militia calling them the Seminoles' "best
soldiers."

By the nineteenth century Black Seminoles had become
key advisors and valuable interpreters for the nation. They
were familiar with English, Spanish, and the Muskogee or
Hitchiti Seminole languages. Not all African runaways from
slavery lived among the Seminoles for some had formed
their own maroon settlements. Against slaveholders, however, all united.

U.S. troops and Greek mercenaries lash the Seminoles left alive, after the destruction of Fort Negro in 1816, back to slavery in Georgia.

The First Seminole War

Georgia slaveholders soon understood that Black Seminole camps could put an end to their slave system. To extinguish this beacon attracting the daring among their slaves, a group calling themselves "Patriots" plotted to annex Florida.

Acting on information that a massive assault was being planned, Seminoles struck first at U.S. plantations. When St. Augustine blacks joined the attack, desertions from plantations began to swell Seminole ranks. With surprise raids Seminoles destroyed a U.S. wagon train, bottled up the Georgia militia, and assassinated the Patriot leader.

President James Madison, who had been giving the Patriot cause covert support, had to withdraw his aid.

But the U.S. slaveholder presence began to undermine the equality between red and black Seminoles. Blacks, though still teachers and advisors, now desperately needed Seminole protection against U.S. slavehunters. The United States, the giant to the north, threatened Seminole land and peace. But for Black Seminole families, liberty itself was at stake.

The U.S., represented by General Andrew Jackson, hero of New Orleans, prepared to wipe out Seminole resistance. Black Seminoles had taken over a British fortress supplied with four cannons, sitting on the Apalachicola River on the Florida panhandle. "Fort Negro" was manned by black officers and men under the direction of Commander Garcia.

Garcia, a lean, tense, tight-lipped man was known for his cunning, courage, and cruelty. He was well-suited to his moment in history. His forces included three hundred Seminole men, women, and children, most of whom were either black or mixed; only thirty-four were pure red Seminoles. Garcia hoped his fortress and troops would shield the Seminole plantations that lined the riverbanks for fifty miles. There peaceful men and women raised crops, tended cattle, and brought up children.

It was clear it would take a miracle to dislodge Garcia and his followers from behind their three-walled fortress. It was situated in a treacherous swamp area impossible to storm. Each month more slaves joined Garcia's band, and to add to his numbers, Garcia's soldiers ventured outside to raid plantations.

Under General Jackson's orders and without a declaration of war, General Gaines marched a massive force of regular U.S. troops, Marines, and five hundred Creek Indian mercenaries. His mission as spelled out by General Jackson was to blow up Fort Negro and "restore the stolen negroes . . . to their rightful owners." The invaders were aided by U.S. Navy ships.

On a hot day in late July 1816, U.S. armed forces and Creeks under Chief McIntosh stood before Fort Negro and demanded its surrender. Garcia's men raised a British flag, and just to antagonize their adversaries, a bloody red flag that dared them to fight. A delegation of Creek leaders sent to receive Garcia's surrender were punched, insulted, and sent back. To make his point Garcia fired off a cannon shot.

A young surgeon with the infantry that day, Marcus Buck, reported, "We were pleased with their spirited opposition, though they were Indians, negroes and our enemies."

It was soon clear, wrote Buck, "most of them determined never to be taken alive."

Each side fired off cannonballs that landed harmlessly in the mud or shallow water. Eight times U.S. ships fired and eight times no one inside Fort Negro was hit. A ninth cannonball, heated red hot in a ship's furnace, landed with miraculous accuracy inside the fort's ammunition dump. In an instant Fort Negro was a roar of flames as hundreds of barrels of gunpowder exploded.

In the smoking ruins the U.S. invaders found 270 dead, three uninjured and sixty-four wounded, some fatally. Garcia, found alive, was executed and the surviving men, women, and children marched back to slavery in Georgia.

The U.S. public heard nothing about this massacre for twenty years. In 1837 New York Judge William Jay broke the story.

The quick U.S. victory on the Apalachicola proved to be the beginning, not the end of Seminole resistance, the first of three Seminole wars that lasted for decades. Even as the invaders rejoiced in a lucky cannon shot, hundreds of Seminole families hurried southeast to join Chief Billy Bowlegs on the Suwannee River.

There they built new homes all the way to Tampa Bay and resumed life as farmers and fishermen, cattle herders and horse breeders. By early 1817 some five hundred red and black Seminoles were drilling, parading to the beat of drums, and preparing for the next battle.

Meanwhile General Andrew Jackson and the James Madison Administration made plans for Florida. General Gaines moved his troops out to burn down the Black Seminole village of Fowltown. Believing it was best for citizens to learn little of the mounting U.S. war in Florida, the U.S. Secretary of War kept Congress in the dark.

By the time President James Monroe took office in 1817, Jackson proposed a secret plan. "Let it be signified to me through any channel that the possession of the Floridas would be desirable to the United States and in sixty days it will be accomplished." Jackson waited patiently for his signal.

In January 1818, Jackson, with two mounted regiments

and a fleet at his command, marched on Billy Bowlegs's towns, "search and destroy" fashion. By May 24, Jackson captured Pensacola, and without a declaration of war, Florida passed into U.S. hands.

Congress greeted Jackson's brash illegality with a mixture of criticism and praise. In 1819 the U.S. paid Spain $5 million for Florida, making Jackson's seizure appear to be a real estate purchase. Now U.S. authorities turned to the "Seminole problem."

From the beginning of its interest in Florida, the U.S. was astounded and infuriated by the easy mixture of races in the Seminole Nation. It constantly sought to divide the two peoples. General Gaines told Seminole King Hatchy, "You harbor a great many of my black people among you at the Suwannee," and asked "to go by you against them." Gaines even promised, "I will not hurt anything belonging to you."

King Hatchy was also definite: "I harbor no negroes. . . . I shall use force to stop any armed Americans from passing my towns or on my lands." Neither side would budge.

For years, the U.S. sent its enormous resources of troops, ships, and military supplies to crush Seminole resistance to its slaveholding way of life. Since it was clear the giant to the north would never accept an independent, armed, and confident free black community inside a slaveholding nation, Seminoles braced for war.

First the U.S. Army drove the Black Seminoles into southern Florida. By 1823, Seminoles had agreed to live on reservations. In 1826, Seminole King Philip (or Emathla) protested: "Here our navel strings were first cut and the blood from them sunk into the earth and made the country dear to us."

To disrupt their racial alliance, U.S. officials promoted slavery among the Seminoles. Of the Five Civilized Nations, only the Seminoles rejected the kind of slavery the U.S. wanted. Wealthy Creeks, who owed their riches to slave labor, were sent to persuade Seminole chiefs to become slave masters. Whites and Creek Indians were encouraged to raid Seminole villages for slaves. Free Seminole men,

This Seminole delegation to Washington, D.C., in 1825 included "Negro Abraham" (center rear) as interpreter and as representative of their large black minority.

women, and children were carried off and sold in southern slave markets.

The position of Black Seminoles, once secure within the nation, now needed strong support from Seminole chiefs. Division entered villages as chiefs argued various courses of action that might leave them in peace. Some Seminole chiefs claimed they now "owned" their black members, since that was the only language whites understood. But some who claimed this ownership took advantage of it and sent their black villagers off to labor hard in their fields.

Seminole law making it impossible to sell a slave remained firmly in place. Seminole chiefs still married black women and had black military and diplomatic advisors. But U.S. policy had begun to erode a strong friendship and trust and to bend equality.

In the face of their changing relations some Black Seminoles left to form their own settlements, and in 1822 the U.S. Secretary of State reported that in Florida there were "five or six hundred maroon negroes wild in the woods." Further south on the peninsula there were even more. Florida now had a growing number of maroons who owed allegiance only to themselves.

For U.S. slaveholders, the armed, uppity Black Seminoles were an intolerable problem. They owned horses, cattle, hogs, and chickens and tended their own gardens. Worse, they were treated as kindly as family members—which they often were. In 1835 U.S. Indian Agent Wiley Thompson reported they had "equal liberty with their owners." They carried guns, were allowed to travel long distances, and acted "impudently" free.

These were not slaves, complained U.S. masters, but people who kept their African names, dressed in fine Seminole clothing and turbans, adopted Seminole stomp dances, sang Seminole and African songs.

In this leniency, slave masters saw a grave threat to their own nearby slave system. Seminole seeds of revolution

This "Authentic Narrative of the Seminole War" drawn in 1836 is shown from the viewpoint of the occupying U.S. armed forces.

might overtake their own plantations and bloody the countryside with racial outbreaks. Florida would not be a fit place for slavery until the Seminole Nation behaved like proper slaveowners.

The Second Seminole War

In 1835 warfare erupted again between U.S. troops and Seminoles. One alleged cause was the seizure by a U.S. officer of Chief Osceola's black wife. Even if this story is more myth than truth, it symbolizes a unity of two races under Osceola's command.

A more basic cause of hostilities was the continued U.S. use of tricks and force to have Seminole chiefs sign treaties agreeing to leave Florida for reservation land in Arkansas and Oklahoma. When Seminole leaders were tricked into signing a treaty, hostilities broke out.

Most alarmed were Black Seminoles. They reasoned that under any U.S. agreement, they would be forced into bond-

age. In December 1835, King Philip led black and red
Seminoles in a raid on a U.S. plantation. Chief Osceola led
a band that murdered a government agent. Another Seminole column wiped out U.S. Major Francis Dade's entire
relief force in the famous Dade Massacre. Florida was again
in flames.

Before this conflict was over, the United States had fought
its most costly Indian war, spending over $40 million and
losing one thousand five hundred soldiers and many
civilians. They battled an enemy one U.S. officer called
"bold, active and armed" and Black Seminoles "more
desperate than Indians." In December 1836, General Sidney
Thomas Jesup, who had recently assumed command of U.S.
forces, decided, "This, you may be assured, is a negro and
not an Indian war."

General Jesup became the first commander to recognize
the crucial role Black Seminoles played in the nation:
"Throughout my operations I found the negroes the most
active and determined warriors; and during the conferences
with the Indian chief I ascertained that they exercised an
almost controlling influence over them."

General Jesup first tried to destroy this alliance by as-
saulting Black Seminole villages and holding their women
and children hostage. He promised Creek mercenaries
"plunder"—meaning captured blacks who could be sold as
slaves. In two months, his troops seized 131 blacks, mostly
women and children. When his men stormed Osceola's
headquarters in January 1837, the chief's personal bodyguard was captured. Of the fifty-five men, fifty-two were
black. Osceola escaped, but illness would end his life in
a year.

By 1837 Osceola had become the leader of black and
red resistance to U.S. slaveholders. While the Seminole
Nation as a whole showed signs of division, those who rode
with Osceola, such as Wild Cat, were prepared to defend
their black brothers and sisters to the death.

Since General Jesup's military operations had not captured one significant Seminole leader to negotiate with, he
worried that his plans would backfire, that Black Seminoles

would lead the nation in full-scale warfare. Worse still, he feared his policies might drive armed Black Seminoles to recruit plantation slaves and throw the countryside into disorder. He believed that Seminole warriors "have fought as long as they had life through the influence of the leading Negroes." For him the key to all negotiations became the Black Seminoles.

Under their own leaders, Negro Abraham and John Horse (or Cohia), and in concert with Chief Osceola and Wild Cat, Black Seminoles pursued their own strategy: Wear down U.S. armed might until compromise was possible. Finally on March 6, 1837, both sides signed a treaty granting that Seminoles keep "their negroes, their *bona fide* property, [and] shall accompany them to the West." Jesup, despite pressure from U.S. slaveholders and their political figures, felt he had no choice: "The negroes rule the Indians, and it is important that they should feel themselves secure; if they should become alarmed and hold out, the war will be resumed."

But General Jesup was not beyond more tricks. When Seminoles furnished hostages to seal the agreement, Jesup planned to let slave traders seize them. Hearing of this betrayal, Wild Cat and Black Seminole leader John Horse led a daring mission that rescued the hostages. At this point Seminole Blacks felt free to circulate around U.S. plantations urging a general uprising against both the U.S. government and the masters.

"All is lost and principally by the influence of the Negroes," Jesup wrote. He now saw that "the two races . . . are identified in interests and feelings" and could not be separated. There was good reason to move Seminoles speedily to the frontier: "Should the Indians remain in this territory, the negroes among them will form a rallying point for runaway negroes from the adjacent states."

Despite his understanding of the racial alliance that dominated the Seminole Nation, General Jesup could not conclude peace. He continued to engage in cruel deceptions that violated the flag of truce, and he seized women and children as hostages. His actions left peace in doubt. In

June 1837 he admitted as much: "We have at no former period in our history had to contend with so formidable an enemy. No Seminole proves false to his country, nor has a single instance ever occurred of a first-rate warrior having surrendered."

Between the General's understanding and his deceptive, militaristic approach lay a sea of gross strategic errors based on race: A U.S. officer and his trained men should be able to defeat a ragged band of ex-slaves and their "savage" allies. No U.S. officer should have to negotiate with such inferiors.

General Jesup faced a dilemma that could not lead to peace. He represented a country that thought Africans were spineless people fit for chains. When captured, such humans were not to be treated as gallant adversaries, but slave runaways. If he forgot these assumptions, his government in Washington and the slaveholders in his camps reminded him.

As the most knowledgeable representative of a giant country, Jesup wanted that victory whites told him was his. But his policies, tactics, and diplomacy were destined to place it beyond his reach.

5

WE ARE ALL LIVING AS IN ONE HOUSE

By late 1837 the U.S. noose was tightening around the Seminole neck, but the Nation showed no willingness to surrender. Those most determined to resist gathered around Osceola and Wild Cat. Still other Florida Seminoles, Africans, and Black Indians set up their own communities as they concluded the United States was untrustworthy. Some escaped to islands in the Caribbean, where slavery had been abolished since 1834.

Others remained in Florida and today some of their offspring claim the peninsula belongs to them, the descendants of the inhabitants who never surrendered.

Conclusion of the Seminole Wars

In the final months of his Florida effort, General Jesup resorted to full-scale deceptions and hostage seizures, and

by the fall of 1837 he had captured King Philip and his
Black Seminole son, John Philip. This brought forth King
Philip's key son, Wild Cat, to negotiate. Riding a spirited
horse, bearing a white crane's plume in his silver headband
as a sign of peace, and accompanied by four chiefs, Wild
Cat arrived to bargain for his father's and brother's release.

For a moment General Jesup wanted to seize him for his
part in the recent hostage rescue success. Instead he decided
to use him to organize a final peace conference. Wild Cat
was sent forth bearing a white flag and asked to return with
leading Seminoles.

His mission changed abruptly when he met his friend,
John Horse. Both men were twenty-five, skilled warriors
and shrewd negotiators. Their friendship would last for
twenty years and revolve around their agreement that red
and black Seminoles were blood sisters and brothers whom
no foe could part. The tall Horse, elegantly attired, towered
above the short, slight Wild Cat. Both had a tendency to

*Coacoochee, or Wild Cat, became the center of red and black
Seminole resistance to U.S. plans in Florida.*

John Horse (or Cohia) joined forces with Wild Cat as his black sub-chief, and together the two men led militant Seminole forces fighting the United States for twenty years.

drink too much, and Wild Cat let this habit interfere with his duties.

The two men saw there was something wrong with asking Seminole leaders to parlay with a foe that did not keep its word. John Horse suggested he alone should go to Fort Peyton to negotiate, and Wild Cat agreed. Horse was able to get Generals Jesup and Hernandez to agree to holding the conference near a Seminole camp. His own betrayal upset, Jesup wrote in his diary that "wherever John [Horse] Covallo was, foul play might be expected."

Then the two generals conspired to seize the entire Seminole peace mission. The Seminoles arrived with many leading figures and the seventy hostages they promised. Osceola was wearing a brightly colored outfit of a blue shirt, red leggings, and a red print shawl around his head, neck, and shoulders.

General Hernandez suddenly ordered the chiefs to deliver "all the Negroes taken from [U.S.] citizens, at once." He made no mention of releasing King Philip and his son. As the Seminoles stood shocked, Hernandez signaled and two hundred U.S. Second Dragoons came out of their forest hiding places, carbines aimed at Seminole hearts.

Prisoners were marched to the old jail at Fort Marion, and thrust into a cell thirty-three-by-eighteen feet to await deportation to Arkansas. Osceola, probably ill with the fever that would soon take his life, slumped in a corner. Wild Cat, John Horse at his side, took command of plans for a breakout.

While Generals Jesup and Hernandez congratulated themselves on a masterful truce violation that captured a dozen Seminole leaders, their prisoners were tearing at a rusted bar blocking a hole atop their eighteen-foot high cell. "We resolved to make our escape or die in the attempt," Wild Cat later wrote. Since the prisoners appeared to accept their fate, a U.S. medical corpsman wrote, "The Indians are perfectly secure and do not dream of escape."

It was weeks before Wild Cat, John Horse, and the others weakened the huge iron bar that blocked the hole. Osceola, at thirty-four, his life slipping fast, took no part.

When a delegation of Cherokees came in to convince the
Seminoles to surrender, Osceola weakly waved "no." During
this time Wild Cat's youngest and oldest brothers were also
captured and thrown in the cell.

Finally, the bar was loosened, and one night twenty
Seminoles, including two women, were led to freedom by
Wild Cat and John Horse. For five days, Wild Cat recalled,
they lived "on roots and berries." On the fifth day they
reached friends who supplied them with food, clothing, and
new weapons. "I'd rather be killed by a white man in
Florida, than die in Arkansas," Wild Cat later wrote.

Colonel Zachary Taylor raced after the fugitives with
70 Delaware Indians, 180 Tennessee volunteer sharpshooters and 800 U.S. soldiers. By the time Taylor's huge
force approached Lake Okeechobee the day before Christmas, dozens of Seminole warriors were hiding in the tall
grass or perched in trees.

The first shot had hardly been fired when the Delawares
deserted. Tennessee riflemen plunged ahead intending to
wipe out the Seminoles and a withering fire brought down
their commissioned officers and then their noncommissioned
officers. The Tennesseeans fled.

When the U.S. regulars were ordered forward, pinpoint
accurate fire brought down, according to Colonel Taylor,
"every officer, with one exception, as well as most of the
non-commissioned officers" and left "but four . . . un-
touched."

Knowing they were no match for hundreds of soldiers,
the Seminoles retreated to waiting canoes and made their
escape. On Christmas Day Colonel Taylor counted 28 U.S.
dead and 112 wounded, and only ten Seminoles dead.

The strongest country in the New World had received a
stunning defeat at the hands of a small band of Black Indian
guerrilla fighters. The battle of Lake Okeechobee became
the most decisive upset the U.S. suffered in more than four
decades of warfare in Florida. But, since the Seminoles had
finally abandoned the battle scene, Colonel Taylor claimed
a victory.

To seek revenge, a furious General Jesup mounted up

Florida maroons continued to battle slave-catchers and the U.S. well into the last century, and some never surrendered their peninsula to foreign rule.

and rode his troops out, but fared little better than Taylor in defeating the Seminoles. Finally, Jesup solemnly promised to negotiate a peace that permitted all Seminoles to migrate together to the Indian Territory in Arkansas and Oklahoma. But he was too late. In May 1838 Jesup was recalled to Washington, his military and peace campaigns a failure. Zachary Taylor, now a brigadier general, assumed the U.S. command in Florida.

It was not until General Worth and 1841 that peace finally came to most of Florida's lush battlefields. "Ten resolute Negroes, with a knowledge of the country, are sufficient to desolate the frontier, from one extent to another," General Worth was told. Not wishing to preside over that dread possibility, he advocated removing all Seminoles before "they become a resort for runaways" and ignite a war "quadruplicate in time and treasure than that now waged." By 1843 most of the Seminole Nation, including five hundred black people, had reached the Indian Territory.

But war in Florida among Seminole holdouts randomly flared up like a fire that had never died. Although in 1844 Wild Cat, John Horse, and other chiefs had traveled to the White House to meet with President Polk, warfare again erupted in the early 1850s and did not end until 1858. For more than forty years men and women in Florida had died trying to live free.

In 1858 a *Harper's Weekly* reporter wrote of a familiar sight:

> The negro slaves are, in fact, the masters of their own red owners. . . . The negroes were the master spirits, as well as the immediate occasion, of the Florida wars. They openly refused to follow their masters if they removed to Arkansas; it was not until they capitulated that the Seminoles ever thought of emigrating.

Life in the Indian Territory

Seminoles arrived in the Indian Territory west of the Mississippi to find themselves at the mercy of a familiar set of enemies. As one of the Five Civilized Nations, they were located on land dominated by the Creek Nation. These ancient foes bitterly resented them for abandoning the old confederation. Surrounded by Creeks, Chickasaws, Cherokees, Choctaws, and whites who practiced a cruel bondage over black people, Seminoles felt pressure at every turn.

The U.S. government spent only three and a half cents a day to feed and clothe each Seminole, and there was little work at first. Wild Cat and John Horse labored hard to feed their people and keep up their sagging spirits. Worst of all, Seminoles became targets of slavehunting raiders, particularly Creeks and whites. Only the reputation of their fighting men kept the nation from being destroyed.

Seminoles were finally given their own section of land, on which they grew crops of corn and rice. These they sold at a good profit. Though they soon convinced their Indian agent they were "high-minded, open, candid and brave people," they were not able to persuade the government to provide them with a school.

In 1849 a pro-slavery faction defeated Wild Cat's bid to lead the nation. For Wild Cat and the Black Seminoles, more was at stake than an election. Once he had envisioned a unity among all red and black people in the southwest, and now he could barely protect his own band of mixed Seminoles.

In 1846 Wild Cat visited Texas three times to meet Kickapoos, Lipans, Apaches, and Tonkawas to discuss his plans. They had listened politely and had not turned him down. Two years later Wild Cat had urged the militaristic Plains Nations to join his Seminoles against Creek, white, and other slavehunters. They did not offer to help.

Little more is known about this grand design than that Wild Cat hoped to establish a military colony for oppressed Indian and black people. He wanted to recruit from the Five Civilized Nations, from Texas and Arkansas plantations, and perhaps elsewhere once his movement gained momentum. Historian Kenneth W. Porter has written: "Wild Cat's ambitions in some respects exceeded those of King Philip, Pontiac and Tecumseh, for he envisioned a union of half a dozen linguistic groups and two races."

In late 1849, the Wild Cat Seminole party received another blow. The U.S. attorney general ruled that Black Seminoles were still slaves under U.S. law. These veterans of many battles to live as one people quietly gathered up and loaded their rifles. Chief John Horse founded the town of Wewoka, moved his families there, and had his crack scouts patrol its boundaries. Intruders, including any who demanded surrender of "slaves," were turned away.

The final blow for the Wild Cat band came when Creeks and U.S. whites demanded that Black Seminoles surrender their guns. At harvest time in 1849, Wild Cat, John Horse, and their followers saddled up and rode toward Mexico. In one night hundreds of Seminoles left the Indian Territory and headed toward the Rio Grande. The United States was moving swiftly toward armed conflict over slavery, and the Seminole Nation was the first to catch fire as the issue heated up.

At the Mexican border Seminole men ferried their women and children across the Rio Grande at Eagle Pass. The men crossed at dawn as armed pursuers galloped into sight and began firing. It was the summer of 1850 and the United States was poised for a decade of bitter conflict over slavery, and finally a war that would pit brother against brother. Becky Simmons, one of the first to cross the river that fateful night, recalled how relieved she was to get "away from de American race people."

At each step of the way to becoming a peaceful agricultural nation, Black Seminoles had been blocked by those seeking slaves. Each time Seminole military strength saved them. Would Mexico finally offer a Seminole Nation peace and land?

The Wild Cat exodus numbered about eight hundred people. Wild Cat also brought some Cherokee and Creek slaves to learn his route to the Rio Grande, and then guide back others. When Wild Cat returned to the Indian Territory in September 1850, he discovered that Black Seminoles who had remained behind were being kidnapped daily by slavehunters.

Creeks, fearful that Wild Cat now meant to lead off their slaves, tried to arrest him. The cagey chief simply announced he had a thousand Kickapoos and others nearby and ready to defend him, and about six hundred armed Creeks turned around and went home.

These Seminoles, in their colorful wedding ceremony costumes, fought for their cultural identity despite unending military conflict and an occupying army.

Twenty Years in Mexico

Wild Cat negotiated for his sovereign nation with President Santa Ana of Mexico. In return for Mexican Army pay and some farmland for their families, Seminole men agreed to serve as "military colonists" along the turbulent Rio Grande border. They dug in at Coahuila province; Wild Cat located below Piedras Negras, and John Horse above it. Their young men became part of Mexico's armed forces, and Wild Cat was appointed a judge and commissioned a colonel.

Seminoles arrived in a country that had ended slavery in 1829 and had welcomed slave fugitives ever since. Some three thousand U.S. blacks lived peacefully in Mexico, most of them far from the Rio Grande border. Periodically, slavehunting posses plunged across the river to seize black people for sale back home. Some Mexican politicians conspired with these desperadoes, the better to finance their political campaigns.

Seminole families had hardly settled down when in 1851 U.S. outlaw John "Rip" Ford rode into Mexico with a band of four hundred men. Wild Cat and John Horse were called upon to drive out the bandits, former Texas Rangers and unemployed Texans. Sixty Seminole fighters drove back the Texans without a casualty. Pleased Mexican officials thanked the Seminoles as "faithful and useful . . . in military operations" and complimented them as "industrious workers."

Relations between Mexico and the U.S. were uneasy and the borderlands dangerous. When John Horse rode to U.S. Fort Duncan to reclaim a horse, he was seized and thrown out by laughing U.S. infantrymen. That year, when the chief was wounded during a shoot-out at Piedras Negras, he was handcuffed and dragged across the border by U.S. ruffians. Wild Cat ransomed Horse for $500, paying in gold stained with blood.

Wild Cat and John Horse worked hard at building good relations with the Mexicans. Black Seminole Rosa Fay remembered: "John Horse would never even let the little children fight with the Mexican children, because he said, 'When we came, fleeing slavery, Mexico was a land of freedom and the Mexicans spread out their arms to us.' "

When Mexicans found fault with Seminole failures to follow army orders, they had a point. Wild Cat and John Horse regularly disregarded orders they considered wrong. Mexican officials complained about Seminole lack of discipline and attention to their authority. But they found this unruly strike force was "always triumphant."

As Seminole fighting men achieved a reputation far and wide for toughness, new recruits—slave runaways from Texas, Black Mexicans, Indian Territory blacks—flocked to their villages. For the nation's elders, the dream of a farming community still remained the great goal.

In 1855 another white invasion force crossed the Rio Grande and captured Piedras Negras. Worried Mexican officials asked Wild Cat and John Horse to assist the Mexican Army. The U.S. forces became bottled up in the city and got a hotter reception than anyone planned when Piedras Negras caught fire. This band of slavehunters, desperadoes, and young men out for fun were lucky to escape back across the Rio Grande.

In 1856 the issue of Seminole refusal to take sides in Mexican politics came up sharply. The ruler of Coahuila ordered John Horse's troops into combat against a political rival. Horse refused. Rosa Fay remembered his position: " 'Here we are,' John Horse would say, 'all living as in one house. How can I take up a gun and kill you, who are my brother, or how can I take up a gun for you and kill that other man, who is also my brother.' "

To explain his decision Chief Horse led a delegation of Seminoles to Mexico City. It was not treason, he said, but neutrality that guided Seminole thinking and action. He and the Seminoles were reprimanded for failing "to render profound respect to the public authorities and to obey their orders." But they were also excused from "taking part in our political dissensions."

Chief Horse's considerable diplomatic skills proved as effective as his military ones. He did not know then that within a year he would need all his personal strength as well.

In late 1856, the U.S. declared that Seminoles were not a part of the Creek Nation, subject to its laws, but independent. This was the signal some of Wild Cat's band had been waiting for, and they packed up for the Indian Territory. Black Seminoles, who would never return to a land of bondage, remained with Wild Cat and some of his followers in Mexico.

Then, in January 1857, nature dealt the remaining Seminoles a cruel blow when smallpox swept through their villages leaving fifty dead. Panicky men and women fled to the woods and hills while others prayed for deliverance. For some, it was a signal that Mexico was more dangerous than the United States. Black Seminoles, with an African immunity, were spared. But the plague carried off Wild Cat, at forty-five, whose force and wisdom had held his Nation together. Becky Simmons recalled the mourning of her people: "Later Wild Cat took sick with de pox and he die. We all was crying fur we done lost him. He was so good."

After Wild Cat's death, his remaining red followers began to trickle back to the Indian Territory. The Black Seminoles were now alone. Becky Simmons remembered, "John Horse . . . [became] our next head man, but dem others been gone back to de territory."

As soldiers guarding the Rio Grande against rustlers and assorted desperadoes of every shade, the Black Seminoles rolled up an impressive record. In 20 battles they captured 432 horses and mules and killed 38 intruders. Not a single Seminole was killed or wounded. Some considered this a miracle.

But the greatest accomplishment of all was the preservation of their Nation as they moved from one country to another.

6

THAT YOU KNOW
WHO WE ARE

For the Black Seminole Nation the Fourth of July, 1870, proved a memorable day. For the white citizens of southern Texas it was a day few would ever forget. Scores of shabbily dressed Seminoles, some on horses carrying infants, and others on foot with their belongings and children, arrived at U.S. Fort Duncan. Led by Snake Warrior, subchief to John Horse, they were the first of three waves of Seminole immigrants to arrive from Mexico over the next eighteen months.

The U.S. Army had sent Captain Frank Perry to Mexico to negotiate an agreement with the Black Nation. In return for its young men serving as scouts for the army, families would be provided with food, necessities, and eventually some good farming land.

The most remarkable fact is that a Black Nation negotiated its entrance into the United States by formal treaty.

It then arrived intact as a Nation, together with its reigning monarch, Chief John Horse.

For both Seminoles and the U.S. Army, this could not have been an easy decision. Black people were voluntarily returning to a country that enslaved their ancestors and then sent armies to crush those who fled their chains. On the army's side, it was hiring men as scouts whom it could not defeat in a century of warfare.

What crucial changes had taken place by 1870 that would make allies of two sworn adversaries? First, the Civil War had ended slavery in the United States, and now black people were forever free. Three Amendments to the Constitution promised equality to ex-slaves, and black men were voting and being elected to office in Texas and nine other southern states. A new day of equal rights was dawning.

The U.S. Army faced hazardous problems in Texas, and these Black Seminole fighters were a powerful answer. Its 4,612 soldiers and officers had to protect 267,339 square miles of mayhem, and guard a restless Rio Grande border. Commanches, Kiowas, Apaches, and various U.S. and Mexican bandit gangs could out-ride and out-fox the Army almost every time.

Worse still, after each surprise, the Army failed miserably at locating or inflicting much damage on their highly mobile foes. This was more than a military problem. For politicians back home victories in the West made good reading for voters and defeats were intolerable.

The Army had a civilian problem as well. Behind their blue-coated backs stood hostile, unreformed southern rebels, who hated the sight of Yankees and their uniforms. When bluecoats battled either Indians or outlaws, it was unclear which side white Texans would cheer.

Somewhere out there, in front of the frontier U.S. Army forts stood groups of cagey native desert fighters the soldiers in blue could not detect, track, or defeat. The Seminole Negro Indian Scouts, as they came to be called in official U.S. records, were hired to even the battle odds.

Major Zenas A. Bliss, desperate for good scouts, sent Captain Perry off to Mexico to sign up these peerless warriors. Seminoles remembered signing this "treaty" with Perry, but the piece of paper, which soon became a bone of contention, disappeared.

The Seminole Negro Indian Scouts

The Black Seminole people arrived on the U.S. side of the Rio Grande like typical immigrants, hoping for their share of iron pots, warm blankets, and good rifles. Like most immigrants to the U.S., they pined for a piece of land they could call their own. Perhaps they assumed that since the U.S. government was prepared to treat them fairly, so would its citizens. They tried to wash the evils of the past from their mind so they would be prepared to enjoy the American Dream.

Texas, as a hotbed of secessionist, racist sentiment, was not about to open its arms to a fiercely independent Black Indian population. People of their color had recently been a salable item in Texas, and most whites regretted this was no longer true. But here was an arrogant, ragged band of Black Indians asking to be treated with respect. This proved too much for white Texans.

The Texas borderlands in the 1870's boasted a savage bloodletting all its own. Discharged Confederate veterans, furious about defeat and the emancipation of their slaves, were still armed and dangerous. Unemployed, they easily became desperadoes spoiling for a fight. This was not a land for the fainthearted or for families with women and children.

The infamous "King" Fisher outlaw gang dominated the Eagle Pass region near Fort Duncan. Cattle-rustling was big business in those parts and John "King" Fisher, handsome and suave, became the most significant political figure in the region. He was not a man you wanted to harbor an active dislike of you.

Almost from the arrival of the Seminole Nation, Fisher decided to challenge Chief John Horse and his men. His gang may have served as the violent cutting edge for those whites who wanted the lands Seminoles had settled.

Though they did not suspect it at first, this last great effort by the Black Seminole people to find peace and land had entered an explosive phase.

Seminole life in Texas began simply enough with seasoned Seminole scouts being trained by green West Point graduates unfamiliar with desert warfare or Seminole ways. The recruits were young men of pure African or mixed Black Indian ancestry in their late teens or early twenties. One, Jim Miller, was said to have "looked white and acted Indian."

In dress, manners, and skills, Seminole men were like Plains Indians. As desert fighters and trackers, they were probably the finest soldiers the U.S. Army ever sent into the field. With their unique skills and record of triumphs over

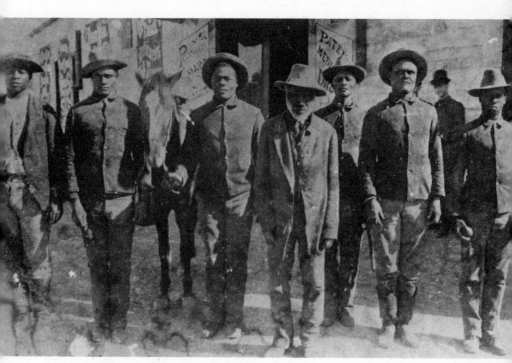

This 1889 photograph of some Seminole Negro Indian Scouts shows both older, retired, and new recruits.

any who crossed their path, they must have approached their new assignment brimming with confidence.

They could maneuver their steeds with grace and wield their rifles with pinpoint accuracy from the saddle. In Mexico they had used slow, muzzle-loading guns. Now the U.S. handed them Spencer carbines, and then the fine Sharps carbines that allowed for smoother, faster loading and firing than any they had ever seen.

The first Seminole-Army tensions began during basic training as white officers tried to impose discipline on these young veterans. These were not eager, inexperienced recruits ready to swallow the army's many rules and regulations. Their monarch had negotiated their hiring as a representative of a sovereign nation. They expected respect.

For their white officers, shock probably came the first time the scouts lined up. Facing the army officers were not neatly dressed, obedient raw recruits, but scruffy men sporting Indian war bonnets, sometimes with buffalo horns. The earliest army reports praise the scouts' fighting abilities but bemoan their appearance—"very poor"—and their clothing —"good enough for Indians."

During the training period, Chief John Horse and his military commander, Snake Warrior, tried to mediate between their scouts and the army brass. The task of finding an officer who could command them and gain their respect was not solved for two years.

The job was finally handed to a young white lieutenant from New York, John L. Bullis. A man of striking contradictions and an unconventional soldier, he proved as tough as his men. Bullis was a Quaker who enlisted as a Union private in the Civil War. As an officer he volunteered to lead black troops. Now filled with traditional army training, he was picked to command the most unorthodox fighting force the U.S. had ever handed rifles.

Clearly a man willing to charge uphill, Bullis had met and married Alicia Rodriguez, a Mexican woman. In Texas, in 1872, this was considered as outrageous as leading Black Indians.

The strong relationship that developed between the short, slight, wiry officer and his scouts made their work unusually effective. Bible in hand, Bullis was invited to Seminole villages to perform marriages and baptisms. Since their own marriage probably did not win them many friends at the fort, the couple may have spent considerable time with the Seminoles.

On the trail Bullis and his scouts quickly became a fighting fist, bold and loyal, risking death for each other. Scout Joseph Philips recalled the relationship in these words:

> The Scouts thought a lot of Bullis. Lieutenant Bullis was the only officer that ever did stay the longest with us. That fella suffer just like we-all did out in de woods. He was a good man. He was an Injun fighter. He was tuff. He didn't care how big a bunch dey was, he went into 'em every time, but he look out for his men. His men was on equality, too. He didn't stand and say, "Go yonder;" he would say "Come on boys, let's go get 'em."

Under Bullis's careful guidance, the Seminole Negro Indian Scouts drove their incomparable skills into the battle against crime in Texas. They could pick up a trail three weeks old, track foes who believed they had eluded all pursuers, and then surprise a target when least expected. On the trail they lived by uncovering hidden springs and eating the rattlesnakes they caught.

They also remained alive by keeping a sharp eye on each other. On April 25, 1875, Bullis, Sergeant John Ward, Trumpeter Isaac Payne, and Private Pompey Factor were tracking a party of twenty-five Commanche rustlers. They came on their quarry and seventy-five stolen horses near the Pecos River at Eagles' Nest. With a daring that bordered on foolishness, the four men challenged the twenty-five.

When the Commanche realized they faced only four, they charged, their Winchester rifle fire driving the scouts back toward their horses. As the Seminoles galloped off, Sergeant Ward turned and saw that Bullis had fallen from his mount and Commanches were closing in on him.

"We can't leave the Lieutenant, boys," Ward shouted and the three scouts wheeled their horses and raced back. As Ward reached Bullis, a bullet cut his carbine sling and another shattered his rifle stock. He reached down and

During their most active campaigns (1873–1882), the scouts were led by white Lieutenant John L. Bullis, a soldier who joined them in protesting their terrible mistreatment by the military bureaucracy.

pulled Bullis up on his horse, and the two galloped away, bullets whizzing past them. "I . . . just saved my hair by jumping on my Sergeant's horse, back of him," Bullis later wrote.

Bullis formally requested that his men each receive the Congressional Medal of Honor. His request was honored and for their valor the three received the highest U.S. military decoration.

End of a Mission

No amount of praise or medals won the Black Seminole Nation its dream of land and a peaceful life. Repeatedly

Chief John Horse led delegations to military authorities and handed in petitions signed by his people. He asked for adherence to treaty obligations, but there was no copy of the disputed treaty.

After three years Seminoles were still squatting on U.S. military reservations at Fort Duncan and Fort Clark close to the Rio Grande. The War Department said it had no land to offer them, and the Department of the Interior claimed they were not entitled to lands granted Indians.

Chief John Horse gathered letters of support from Lieutenant Bullis, Major Bliss, General C. C. Auger (commander, Department of Texas), and General Philip Sheridan, Civil War hero. Neither petitions, pleas, nor letters of support melted any bureaucratic hearts in Washington.

To make matters worse, the army high command issued orders that cut Seminole rations. Food and necessities for about fifty scouts were spread among three hundred men, women, and children. Soon a proud nation was reduced to foraging for food, stealing stray cattle, and taking jobs in white homes. Some scouts left for Mexico with their families, and their places were taken by eager Afro-Americans, Mexican Seminoles, and other red and black Indians.

As a fighting unit the Seminole Negro Indian Scouts rolled up an impressive record guarding the Texas frontier against intruders. By a miracle they suffered no casualties. Scout Bill Daniels believed that when "you are fighting for the right . . . God will spread His hand over you."

But there was no one to protect the Seminoles from the very white Texans they guarded. John "King" Fisher made it his goal to drive off the Black Seminoles and assassinate their monarch, Chief Horse. Besides resenting the proud black fighters, he probably objected to the war on crime they fought in the Eagle Pass region where his rustler gang roamed.

Fisher boasted he had killed a man for every year of his life "not counting Mexicans." With their carbines and six-shooters, his outlaws dominated politics, business, and life in general in the region.

By Christmas 1874, trouble between King Fisher's desperadoes and the Seminoles boiled over. There was a shoot-out in a Bracketville saloon and Corporal George Washington, Chief Horse's nephew, was fatally wounded in the stomach. Another bullet creased King Fisher's scalp, leaving him shaken but even more determined to settle matters with guns.

To halt the bloodshed before it became open warfare, the Army moved the Black Seminole Nation to Fort Clark, which was further from Bracketville than Fort Duncan was. But if anyone believed that mere distance would satisfy the outlaws, they were wrong.

The Seminoles found farming and living conditions at Fort Clark more pleasant than Fort Duncan. But no sooner had they settled down than they learned that Kinney County whites wanted their new land. And the King Fisher gang stood ready to push any dispute with Black Seminoles into a shooting war.

In the spring of 1876, Chief Horse and scout Titus Payne were peacefully riding near an army hospital when they were ambushed. Payne was dead by the time he hit the ground. John Horse was badly wounded, as was his horse, American. But American was able to pull the injured chief to safety, probably saving his life.

By now Seminoles may have felt themselves at sea among weak friends and deadly enemies. Local whites wanted them removed from lands they farmed and local outlaws wanted them dead. The army paid for their services as scouts but drastically reduced their rations and refused to grant them land promised in a treaty. Their friends, from powerful generals down, signed their petitions, but no one in Washington cared anyway. Seminole fighting men could defeat any foe, but no one could protect innocent people from cowardly ambushes.

By this time a sturdy nation may have become deeply divided over their stay in the United States. Some families gave up and returned to Mexico.

For many huddling in the temporary village outside Fort Clark, the last straw came during the early morning of a New Year's Eve dance in 1877. A local sheriff and his deputies rode out to arrest Adam Payne in connection with the murder of a black soldier.

Payne had a reputation as a tough man and had earned a Congressional Medal of Honor. The sheriff may have planned his next move or just lost his courage. At any rate he did not arrest Payne, but blasted him from behind with a shotgun—at such close range that Payne's clothes caught fire.

This pointless violence sent shock waves through the entire community, and five scouts, led by Pompey Factor, immediately packed up and rode off to the Rio Grande. They paused only to wash the dust of Texas from their horses' hooves, and then continued on into Mexico.

The majority of the scouts remained loyal if not to the U.S. government, at least to Bullis and their jobs. New re-

Pompey Factor, one of four scouts to earn the Congressional Medal of Honor, died penniless in his mid-eighties, denied a U.S. Army pension.

cruits were no longer from the original Black Seminole Nation. More and more they came from Texas Afro-Americans, former black U.S. soldiers, and black Mexicans.

By 1882 Bullis and his scouts had virtually pacified a terrifying no man's land. That year a dozen army expeditions from Texas Army posts covered 3,662 miles and found no raiders of any kind. In eleven years, twenty-six expeditions, and twelve major engagements, Bullis and his desert fighters had not lost a man in battle or had one seriously wounded.

They frightened off the most dangerous scorpions and brought law and order to a land known for marauding killers. Bullis was honored as "The Friend of the Frontier" by Texans, and later became a brigadier general in the army. He was presented with two handsome swords by appreciative local citizens and listed in *Who Was Who in America*. He was once called "the greatest Indian fighter in the history of the United States Army."

His wife Alicia died young, and Bullis remarried and settled down in San Antonio. He died in 1911 of a heart attack.

Death of a Nation

The brave Seminole Negro Indian Scouts did not share in this glory. Although the unit was not formally dissolved until 1914, it had lost heart earlier, on the night Adam Payne was murdered.

In 1882 an aging John Horse undertook a final mission for his land-hungry people. He rode his horse American out of Texas into Mexico. According to one of his followers, he was "hunting for a place to live, for a home—he was always doing that." The gracious reigning Seminole monarch was never seen again.

For a piece of the American Dream, he and his people had pinned their hopes on a return to a United States free of slavery. Some had given their last full measure of devotion, and none had received their due or their land.

Pompey Factor as a young private helped save the life of

Lieutenant Bullis, and received the Medal of Honor. But years later he could not even get an army pension. In his late seventies and still carrying the empty case that once held his medal, he asked a Texas lawyer to plead his case before the Army brass. It was no use. The Army responded that it had no record of his service.

Two years later, in 1928, Pompey Factor died and was buried in Bracketville, Texas. His funeral expenses of $86.40 were paid by a friend because he died penniless and without an army pension.

Today the remaining members of the Black Seminole Nation are distributed on both sides of the Rio Grande border near Eagle Pass, scene of their greatest triumphs and disasters. They are largely part of the region's dark poor, their historic valor still unrecognized.

There is no monument to Seminole courage and audacity anywhere in this country. In 1970 a Seminole Negro Indian graveyard outside Bracketville was set aside to mark the

This photograph shows the marker at the Seminole cemetery in Texas.

final resting place of Pompey Factor, Isaac Payne, Adam Payne, and other people who had no rest while they were alive. They should have earned more than that late gesture to their fallen heroes.

Is there any group in history that, beginning before 1776 and stretching from one generation into the next for more than a century—and reaching from Florida's marshlands to Texas's deserts—fought harder for liberty and justice in the Americas?

The last word about the Black Seminole Nation should rest with its historic figure, Chief John Horse. In December 1873 he and Snake Warrior walked into General Augur's office and entered a plea for "my people" to "have a home." In his most diplomatic language the chief reminded the general he had fought almost a dozen U.S. generals in Florida. He had negotiated with General Taylor who became a U.S. president and with President James Polk in Washington.

Still identifying himself as part of "the Seminole Wild Cat Party," his words were taken down by an Army scribe and sent on to the adjutant general in Washington. John Horse's oral petition is on file in the National Archives. This is part of what he said:

> . . . I want full rations for my people, please if so granted, and I like to have the Mexicans who are intermarried with my people, and which are with us, and good men, may be enlisted for scouting.
>
> . . . I say for my people that the President of the United States may grant us what the Fathers before God have promised us; and I come here, General Augur, to present you all this, that you know who we are.
>
> General, I come here to make a new treaty, and the wish I ask for please grant Sir; the same time I want to see all my children have their right, as I brought them all here. . . .
>
> We come here not to tell a lie, but to tell the whole truth, and that you do all for us you can to have a home. . . .
>
> *John Horse*
> his *x* mark

7

HE WAS OUR GO-BETWEEN

For the earliest Europeans, the Americas were truly a land of opportunity. They came from a continent torn with religious strife. Its kings, nobles, and merchants regularly dragged their people into land and sea wars. The plight of ordinary men and women was terrible. About 2 percent of the population owned 95 percent of the land. Common folk wallowed in poverty and want, without hope or security. They were forced into labor battalions or conscript armies.

Everywhere a rigid intolerance held sway. Europeans lived by a rural British slogan: "He's a stranger, hit him on the head!"

These Europeans greeted the people of the Americas with hostility and a lust for profit. In dealing with non-Christians, they saw little reason to observe common rules of fair play, and rarely did. They tramped into the American wilderness with a Bible, a musket, and a diplomacy that knew no rules.

As Native Americans learned that European diplomacy spoke with a forked tongue, new approaches were necessary. At times the foreigners used their African slaves to represent their interests or serve as ambassadors of good will. Like the Indians, Africans had a tradition of keeping promises and treaty obligations. As slaves, they welcomed an opportunity to represent their own interests while they were advance agents for a powerful new order.

Some Africans became more than peacemakers, negotiators, and bridges between cultures in the wilderness. They began to identify with their new friends of the hills, streams, and mountains. A few wrote unheralded chapters in New World diplomacy.

Estevanico

It is an irony that the first explorer from the Old World to enter Arizona and New Mexico's free, vast expanses was himself a slave. But Estevanico was a highly unusual individual who left a confused legacy. Even his name poses a question. Since he was called Estevanico or Little Stephen, was he a tall, even gigantic "Little Stephen," or an unusually small "Little Stephen"?

Not too much is known of his early life. Born in Azamore, Morocco, around 1500, he was probably made captive as a teen-ager when Portugal's King Manoel seized the city in 1513. His life is a blank until June 17, 1527. Then he emerged as a bearded young man, the slave of a Spaniard, Andrés Dorantes, as the two board a ship at Sanlúcar de Barrameda, Spain, for the New World.

The Spaniard and the Moroccan had hardly landed in exotic Hispaniola when they joined an expedition to explore Florida. In 1528 King Ferdinand ordered the exploration and his newly appointed Governor of Florida, Pánfilo de Narváez, personally led it.

Some five hundred Spaniards and their African slaves set out on an adventure none would ever forget. From the moment of their first landing at Sarasota Bay the effort skidded toward catastrophe. They quickly ran out of food and then patience. Spaniards, used to a pleasantly warm climate, had to contend with tropical rainstorms, wild animals, jungles, and quicksand. Starvation drove desperate men toward madness. Some ran off seeking salvation in the treacherous countryside, others prayed in vain and many died hungry and lost.

By the time the explorers reached a Native American village they counted only eighty survivors. Their calamities had just begun. While the exhausted men rested, disease struck, leaving only fifteen survivors. Narváez and his men named this place "Misfortune Island" and pushed on.

Bad luck continued to stalk the foreigners. Death carried off Narváez and, one by one, most of the others. Soon of the original five hundred adventurers only Andrés Dorantes, Estevanico, Cabeza de Vaca, and one other Spaniard remained alive.

Alone in a terrifying land they barely understood, the four shared hardship and terror. At one point they were made slaves of separate Indian Nations, but during a meeting of their masters, they made good an escape. They were destined to spend eight years wandering.

A diary of their sojourn was kept by their leader, Cabeza de Vaca. It told of Estevanico's crucial role whenever Indians appeared. He posed as a medicine man and magic healer, and the other three followed his lead. Estevanico found success reciting improvised prayers and making signs over ill and dying Indians. For this service the four were rewarded with food, water, and directions. As the most skilled magic healer, Estevanico was able to gain valuable information and necessities from grateful Native Americans.

Further, as they made their way from one native village to another, the African picked up languages from and instilled confidence in those he met. De Vaca's account records that it was Estevanico who "was our go-between; he informed himself about the ways we wished to take, what towns there were, and the matters we desired to know."

By now Estevanico was beginning to hear, along with other information, wild tales about rich Cibola, or "The Seven Cities of Gold." The Spaniards shared the excitement

The foreign discovery of Arizona and New Mexico by Estevanico was captured in this mural by Jay Datus.

when Indians insisted that somewhere north of Mexico lay a city made of gold and silver. This was the glittering wealth Spain had hoped to find in the New World.

In 1536 the four shabby survivors staggered into Spanish headquarters in Mexico. They brought with them the first great folk myth of the Americas—the tale of Cibola. After the three Spaniards recovered from their ordeal and regained some weight, they left for Spain. Not even the lure of gold and silver could hold them.

Estevanico did not have that choice, and he was sold to the Viceroy of Hispaniola, Antonio de Mendoza. The governor kept his slave guest talking about Cibola's riches, and Estevanico produced some bright metal objects natives had given him to prove that smelting was an art practiced in Cibola.

In 1538 Governor Mendoza organized an expedition to discover this land of great wealth and picked Father Marcos de Niza, a Franciscan friar, to lead it. Estevanico was his advance scout and advisor.

The African was sent ahead with a few Indians and two greyhounds and was directed to send back accounts of his progress toward Cibola. The closer he came or the more information he gathered, the faster he would contact Father de Niza. The unusual method of communication chosen by the priest was a cross. The closer Estevanico came to Cibola, the larger the cross to be sent back.

Heading northwest from Mexico, Estevanico employed his experience as a translator and his guise as a medicine man. He carried a large gourd decorated with a string of bells and one red and one white feather to symbolize a search for peace and friendship. Indian men and women— as many as three hundred—joined his party and adorned him with jewelry and gifts.

Estevanico began to send back crosses to indicate progress, each larger than the last. His Indian messengers told Father de Niza of his scout's large following and rapid strides. Enthusiasm mounted as the priest urged a faster pace to reach Cibola, just behind Estevanico.

Then, suddenly, there was no word from the African— no messengers, no crosses. The rest of the expedition stopped and waited tensely. Finally, two wounded Indians staggered into the priest's camp. They told a story of terror, death, and sorrow. Estevanico and his followers were approaching a village near Cibola when they were attacked. The party scattered, some captured, others slain.

Estevanico? "We think they have shot him to death," the Indians said. "We are the only survivors."

The story of Estevanico here becomes conjecture and argument. Some historians, unfriendly toward the African, claim he abused Indian women and cheated their men, so he was murdered. One scholar believes Estevanico died for claiming to represent a powerful white country to Indians. Some historians have wondered if the young slave saw an opportunity for freedom and took it.

Perhaps he created a clever cover story—"We think they have shot him to death"—and made good his escape.

The Zuñi Nation, whose pueblos he was approaching at the end, told a folk legend into the twentieth century about a brave Black Mexican—a large man, with "chilli [thick] lips" who was "killed by our ancestors."

No one ever found the Seven Cities of Gold, but Estevanico's efforts led to the first thorough exploration of the American southwest by Coronado and others. The African's command of languages, his ability to win Native Americans' confidence, stand in sharp contrast to the brutality of some European adventurers. Bold and persuasive, and with some tricks up his sleeve, Estevanico succeeded mainly through a sensitive human touch.

Jean Baptiste Point Du Sable

It is unclear whether Estevanico lived happily with the native people of Arizona or New Mexico or died at their hands. The story of a fur trapper named Du Sable leaves no doubt that this handsome black Frenchman married into and remained a good friend of the Illinois Indians.

He also maneuvered with the skill of an experienced diplomat as Illinois slipped from French to British to U.S. control. His personal charm and diplomacy kept him from being jailed as an enemy agent and won him powerful white and Indian allies.

There are gaps in his early life. Du Sable was born somewhere in the Caribbean in 1745 to a French sailor father and an African slave woman. Sent to Paris for an education, he ended up in the Illinois Territory in 1779. With him came twenty-three French art treasures and a desire to become a fur trapper.

As a Frenchman in a land recently taken by the British, Du Sable fell under suspicion. On July 4, 1779, a British officer complained he "was much in the interest of the French" and Du Sable was arrested for "treasonable intercourse with the enemy." He managed to escape only to be arrested again. This time he so impressed British Governor Patrick Sinclair that Du Sable was released and for five years placed in charge of a settlement on the St. Charles River.

Du Sable had no difficulty in persuading local Indians

Jean Baptiste Pointe du Sable's portrait by the French artist Raoul Yarin was sketched in 1930.

he was a friend. It took much longer for white Chicagoans to recognize that Du Sable was their city's founder.

Du Sable entered the fur trading business and married a Potawatomi woman named Catherine. Their friends included a host of people, among them Chief Pontiac and Daniel Boone. One can only wonder what rough frontiersmen and Indians thought when they first entered the Du Sable home and saw its display of French works of art. The couple also purchased and developed some eight hundred acres of land in Peoria, but Chicago was their great love and they lived there for sixteen years.

Their trading post became prosperous and the Du Sables soon had a son and a daughter. Centrally located, their store and home attracted many trappers and swelled to include a forty by twenty-foot log cabin, a bakehouse, a dairy, a smoke house, a poultry house; a workshop, a barn, and a mill. Du Sable made a living as a trader, but was also a miller, a cooper, and a farmer.

The Du Sables became devout Catholics and in 1798 were formally married in a church ceremony. They were delighted when, two years later, their daughter married another Frenchman in a Catholic ceremony.

Jean and Catherine, although doing well, sold off twenty-one of his French paintings, perhaps to finance his next career move. He announced his candidacy for chief of a local Indian Nation at Mackinac, but he lost the election.

As the couple grew older they decided to sell their Chicago home and move in with their daughter's new family in St. Charles, Missouri. For the property and houses alone, they received $1200, and they also sold thirty head of cattle, thirty-eight pigs, two mules, and many chickens.

When Catherine died in 1800, the founder of Chicago began to worry about his future. He did not want to die penniless or to be buried in any but a Catholic cemetery. Though, in 1814 he did have to file bankruptcy papers, he was laid to rest four years later in St. Charles Borromero Roman Catholic Cemetery.

York

York, the slave of William Clark of the famous Lewis and Clark expedition, may not have conceived of himself as an ambassador of good will to foreign nations. As a slave he was pleased to share this great adventure in the wilderness. Besides, he was too busy developing some striking frontier skills, learning new Native languages and making friends among the strange people he met. But ambassador of good will he became, and a vital asset to the famous exploration of the Louisana Territory.

York was born around 1780 to house slaves of the Clark family in Virginia and grew up as the special friend of their son William, York's age. Slaveowning families permitted and sometimes encouraged their sons to take a good friend from among their slaves to share their youthful adventures. Each young man just had to remember clearly what his station in life was. In 1799 Clark inherited the family estate, and this included ownership of his childhood companion, York.

The two men were twenty-three when President Thomas Jefferson purchased Louisiana from Napoleon. Since no one knew what lay in this vast land that stretched from the Mississippi to the Pacific, the President asked his secretary Meriwether Lewis to lead an exploring party. Lewis promptly chose his friend Clark, and Clark just as quickly decided to bring along York. By this time York was an imposing man, six feet in height and weighing over two hundred pounds—in an age when most men were under five foot six.

In St. Louis, where the expedition trained for the trip, York began to pick up French and Indian words. By the time the task force set out, he was able to assist Sacagewea, the Shoshone woman, in translations. For the next two and a half years, the two dark explorers were able to convince one Native American Nation after another that the forty-three men and one woman came in peace.

York also became one of the party's best hunters, fishermen, and scouts. By the last year of the journey he was given the assignment of trading with the Indians for the expedition's food.

York was able to bring into his diplomacy more than his considerable frontier skills, command of language, and smiling good will. He was incredibly fast on his feet and utilized his agility and exotic looks when negotiating. Many Native Americans had never seen an Afro-American before, certainly none of his size and strength. Clark's diary recorded how the Arikara "all flocked around him and examined him from top to toe." York responded to this attention by showing "his powers of strength" and telling the astonished Arikara that he had once been a "wild animal." His leaping agility won new friends for the expedition.

All the way to the Pacific coast, Clark wrote, Indian

women were "very fond" of York. Like other members of
the force, York took Indian "wives" in the various villages
they visited.

Among the Mandan Indians on the Upper Missouri,
York leaped and danced his way into hearts, startling people
that so "large a man should be so active" and agile.
Fascinated by their black visitor, some Mandan villagers
decided to rub York's black skin with a wet finger to see if

*York meets the Mandan Indians of the northwest, as seen in this
painting by the noted artist Charles Russell. The Mandans are
rubbing York's skin to see if his color will come off, an incident
reported in Lewis and Clark's notes of the historic expedition to the
Pacific and back.*

the color would come off. Artist Charles M. Russell captured this moment in a famous painting.

More than the bright trinkets the explorers had brought to gain Indian attention, Shoshone, Nez Percé, and other nations along the Columbia River found York fascinating. York diplomatically turned this fascination into a bargaining tool, and he became a skilled negotiator.

By the end of 1805, Sacagewea and York had earned an equal voice in the expedition and were asked to vote with the others on the location of a winter camp. York had leaped far from slavery in Virginia.

Once a Flathead Indian tried to explain how his people saw York: "Those who had been brave and fearless, the victorious ones in battle, painted themselves in charcoal. So the black man, they thought, had been the bravest in the party."

Upon the expedition's return to St. Louis, everyone packed up and headed for home and rest. Clark brought his slave back to Kentucky and dull routine. When Clark was appointed Governor of the Missouri Territory and Director of Indian Affairs, York went with him. He hired out near Louisville so he could be near his wife, who worked for a white family.

Clark eventually liberated York and gave him a wagon and six horses. With these he ran a transportation business between Nashville and Richmond. But the explorer saw his business go from bad to worse, and York eventually died of cholera.

Perhaps when one is lifted from slave life in Virginia to hack a unique path through the wilderness, the rest of life seems very dull. When one creates an original brand of frontier negotiation and deals effectively with Native Americans for an expedition authorized by President Jefferson, running a team of horses hardly compares.

8

THEIR MIXING IS TO BE PREVENTED

In Latin America, Africans had found excellent places to hide and many Indians to aid them. Europeans were reluctant to seek out these remote hideouts. In North America, Africans were not that lucky.

To begin with, there were fewer Indians. The largest body of Native Americans east of the Mississippi, the Iroquois Confederacy, never numbered more than sixteen thousand men, women, and children. There were no rugged mountains, impenetrable jungles, and few hidden havens for runaways. Slaves who ran to the forests and hills found fewer red hands of friendship, and little military support from those who did help. Daring fugitives could reach Indians in the backwoods, but so too could slavehunters and their tracking dogs.

British America

On both northern and southern American continents, Europeans enslaved Africans and Native Americans and drove both hard to pile up profits in the shortest possible time. This led to laws and policies that were genocidal toward Indians and just short of that for Africans. In North America, the British added a new element to their relationship with nonwhites. It was a curious, sharp feeling of personal contempt—today we call it "racism." It often seemed as important for the English to emphasize the "inferiority" of dark people as it was to make a profit.

British merchants, missionaries, and soldiers quickly penetrated Native American villages with their beliefs and businesslike approach to life. By 1670 Indian men were using axes and hoes, wearing hats, shoes, stockings, breeches, and linen shirts, and carrying hatchets and knives made in England. Native women were using jewelry, brass kettles, thread, needles, scissors, petticoats, calico, lace, and mirrors produced across the Atlantic. Native Americans fought enemies with flints, muskets, powder, and bullets purchased from European merchants. They had become dependent on their white foes.

An erosion of native culture followed. People who worshiped nature began to practice the Christian religion of their enemies. Those who cared little for private gain and practiced cooperation in economic life were taught "everything has a price." From the first exchange of trinkets for land, muskets for corn, and Christianity for a native faith in nature, an entire culture was being directed toward a European love of possession.

Since labor was in short supply in British America, the earliest colonists enslaved first Indians and then Africans. Since unending bondage did not exist in English law, the first form was called "indenture" and lasted for about seven years. "Indentured servants" of any color could be mistreated while in service, have their personal life regulated, and their time extended by scheming masters.

Since all three races were abused under this system, they

often rebelled and escaped. Reward notices of the time tell of red, black, and white men and women fleeing their masters—sometimes together.

The first Africans introduced into Jamestown's economy in 1619 became indentured servants, not slaves. Upon their release, they became part of the Virginia colony. Some became landowners, and one, Anthony Johnson, ruled an African community of twelve homesteads and two hundred acres in Virginia's Northampton County.

In the 1630s the rules of indenture began to change. It became legal to hold Africans or Indians for more than the usual seven years, even for life. The change began on the English-ruled island of Barbados when the governor announced "that Negroes and Indians . . . should serve for life, unless a contract was made to the contrary." And beginning in 1636, only whites received contracts of indenture.

British America had taken a large step in dividing labor by race and reserving the worst for dark people. More and more white laborers were pouring into the thirteen British colonies, and masters did not want them making common cause with Africans or Native Americans. Masters had probably concluded their profitable labor system would work only as long as whites did not see their condition and fate as identical with nonwhites.

In 1636 a Massachusetts Indian became the first North American to be legally enslaved, sentenced to work until he died. A decade later Governor John Winthrop thought of the idea of seizing Narragansett Indians to exchange for Africans. Around the same time British commissioners meeting in New Haven also decided that it was fair to make slaves of Indians and exchange them for Africans.

By 1661 slavery had become legal in the British colonies. Africans were preferred because of being thousands of miles from home. Indian slaves were able to flee to their armed brothers and sisters—and then come roaring back seeking revenge.

This idea of keeping slaves distant from their homes and families was crucial to having them under strict control. British merchants took Indians enslaved on the mainland and shipped them out to the West Indies. This was the only safe way to enslave Native Americans, for bondage was only secure when its victims felt they had no one to turn to, no friends nearby.

Reward notices in colonial newspapers now told of African slaves who "ran off with his Indian wife" or "had kin among the Indians" or is "part-Indian and speaks their language good."

In slave huts and beyond the British settlements along the coast, African and Native American women and men shared their sorrows and hopes, their luck and courage. They did not always know where to run to, but they knew where to run from.

Judging from reward notices, Africans picked up Indian languages as soon as they reached a frontier region. Runaways in the woods always needed outside help.

The first full-scale battle between Native Americans and British colonists took place in Jamestown, Virginia, in 1622. Africans fared a lot better than their owners. According to historian James H. Johnstone "the Indians murdered every white but saved the Negroes." This, noted Johnstone, became a common pattern during wars between colonists and Indians.

British colonial law not only lumped Native American and African people together, but handed both worse punishments than whites. A Virginia law set twenty-five lashes for whites who stole pigs, but increased this to thirty-nine lashes if the accused were a red or black person. Virginia soon declared "Negro, Mulatto and Indian slaves . . . to be real estate."

Beginning slowly in 1670, rules of bondage began to change to permit Native Americans to leave. Virginia began matters that year by stating that Indians were enslaved for only twelve years, Africans for life.

This decision was based on a peculiar legal point that Africans were "imported into this colony by shipping" and Indians came "by land." No mention was made of the fact that Indians did not come by land, but had lived there before English settlers arrived, or that most Africans had been living in Virginia for much longer than most British citizens.

Before Indians were eased out of the slave system, they had lived and married with African slaves, and produced in their offspring a new class of Americans held in chains. When the slave codes talked of "Indian slaves," it probably meant those Black Indians. For example, although New York's Assembly banned Indian bondage in 1679, in 1682 it forbad "Negro or Indian Slaves" from leaving their masters' homes or plantations without permission. The next year the Assembly denied "Negro or Indian Slaves" from meeting anywhere together in groups of four or more or being armed "with guns, Swords, Clubs, Staves or Any Other kind of weapon."

Between 1619 and 1700 labor in North America had become divided by skin color. Liberty itself would remain divisible by skin color through the American Revolution and up to the Civil War and emancipation.

This division kept working people in America from uniting against an unjust labor system. Masters deported Indian slaves to the West Indies so they could not flee to their homes and loved ones. They enlisted whites and local Indians to help them hunt their runaway African slaves. When local Native Americans refused this work, they reached out to Indians on distant islands who needed money or trade. Through this cleverness, slaveowners hoped to sleep soundly each night and awake each day to greater profits.

The Southern Frontier

To an extent not revealed in Hollywood frontier movies, slave labor built the earliest European communities in the south. From 1690 to 1720, Africans cleared land, introduced African rice culture, navigated river vessels, and delivered the mail in the Carolinas. Only the most trustworthy slaves were brought to the frontier, and most stood by their masters. But some fled to the woods and Indians at the first opportunity, giving their owners something more to worry about.

For British subjects the question of bringing slaves so close to the frontier and Native Americans stirred a lively debate. A South Carolina law of 1725 imposed a £200 fine on those who brought their slaves to the frontier. A British colonel urged enforcement "because the Slaves . . . talk good English as well as the Cherokee language and . . . too often tell falsities to the Indians which they are apt to believe." In 1751, another law warned "The carrying of Negroes among the Indians has all along been thought detrimental, as an intimacy ought to be avoided."

But sound racial policies on the frontier clashed with the desire to reap the profits produced by slave labor. Virginia surveyor George Washington, twenty-three, urged the use of "mulattoes and Negroes . . . as pioneers and hatchet men" in the wilderness. An early print shows a young Washington with a black and white surveying team.

George Washington, who advocated bringing Afro-Americans to the frontier despite their proximity to Native Americans, is shown in Virginia with a black and white surveying team.

British colonists tried to play one dark race against the
other on the southern frontier. The Maryland Assembly in
1676 offered Indians rewards for recapturing slave runaways. In South Carolina, in 1708, 5,280 European settlers
tried to watch over 2,900 African and 1,400 Indian slaves.
Europeans sent slave "cattle hunters" to protect Charleston
from Indian raids. In 1740 South Carolina offered Indians
£100 for each slave runaway captured alive, £50 for
"every scalp of a grown negro slave."

The conflict among the three races on the frontier had
each side seeking allies wherever they could be found.
During the Yemassee War of 1715, Natchez Indians
murdered whites and seized their slaves. When the British
ordered one thousand two hundred soldiers against the
Natchez, they sent black troops along. And when Governor
Charles Craven of South Carolina confronted the Natchez's
army he found it also included armed black prisoners.

By 1729 the frontier racial cauldron was boiling over in
South Carolina and Louisiana. Slaves rose in rebellion at
Stono, South Carolina. Terrified whites turned to Catawbas
Indians, noted for their slavehunting skills, to recapture or
slay all rebels. In Louisiana, the governor was shocked to
learn Chickasaws had contacted a daring band of Banbara
Africans enslaved at New Orleans. His spies told him the
two peoples plotted an insurrection that would kill whites
and create a red-black maroon confederacy.

Hardly had he solved this threat when he heard New
Orleans was menaced by Chouchas Indians a few miles
north. The governor sent off armed black slaves to carry
out a massacre.

These sporadic conflicts hardly matched the unending
racial disturbances along the border between British
Georgia and Spanish Florida. Spain relied largely on the
blacks and Indians of Florida to resist any invasion by slavehunting British. When Georgia Governor Oglethorpe invaded Florida in 1740, Spain's red and black troops repelled
him. Oglethorpe learned that two hundred Africans, including many ex-slaves from Georgia, guarded St. Augustine.

When Spain ordered a counterattack on Georgia in 1742,
their armed forces included a black regiment and "negro

commanders clothed in lace" bearing the same rank as white officers. The British concluded they had more to worry about from this force starting a slave revolt in Georgia than from anything Spanish troops might do.

At around this time British colonists in the southern colonies began introducing the practice of African slavery among neighboring Native Americans. They concentrated on the Five Civilized Nations—Cherokees, Chickasaws, Choctaws, Creeks, and Seminoles—as the largest body of Indians present on their borders. Their aim was to make their slave property more secure by making Indians partners in the system. Indians who accepted slavery would not take in runaways fleeing European masters.

Except for the Seminoles, the Five Civilized Nations began to accept the foreign idea of slavery. Even so, their idea of how it should work differed from British practices. Quaker slaveholder John Bartram, botanist to the king of England, visited some Indian owners in 1770. He found their slaves dressed better than the chief, married into the

Cherokees had thousands of black members, most of whom had been introduced to the Nation as slaves by whites seeking to make bondage universal.

nation easily, and their children were "free, and considered in every respect equal" to other members. After a visit to the Creeks, Bartram wrote:

> I saw in every town in the Nation I visited captives, some extremely aged, who were free and in as good circumstances as their masters; and all slaves have their freedom when they marry, which is permitted and encouraged [and] they and their offspring are in every way upon an equality with their conquerers.

But how did Native Americans view the way Europeans treated their African prisoners? Two European missionaries, trying to convert the Delaware Nation, returned rejected but with this report on the Delaware response to their plea:

> They rejoiced exceedingly at our happiness in thus being favored by the Great Spirit, and felt very grateful that we had condescended to remember our brethren in the wilderness. But they could not help recollecting that we had a people among us, whom, because they differed from us in color, we had made slaves of, and made them suffer great hardships, and lead miserable lives. Now they could not see any reason, if a people being black entitled us then to deal with them, why a red color should not equally qualify the same treatment.
>
> They therefore had determined to wait, to see whether all the black people amongst us were made thus happy and joyful before they would put confidence in our promises; for they thought a people who had suffered so much and so long by our means, should be entitled to our first attention; and therefore they had sent back the two missionaries, with many thanks, promising that when they saw the black people among us restored to freedom and happiness they would gladly receive our missionaries.

Despite every European effort to keep one dark people from assisting the other, the two races began to blend on a vast scale. Black Indians were apparent everywhere if one bothered to look. Thomas Jefferson, for example, found among the Mattaponies of his Virginia, "more negro than Indian blood in them." Another eyewitness reported Virginia's Gingaskin reservation had become "largely African." Peter Kalm, whose famous diary described a visit to the British colonies in 1750, took note of many Africans living with Indians, with marriage and children the normal result.

That same year a Moravian missionary, J. C. Pyrlaeus, visited the Nanticoke Nation on Maryland's eastern shore to compile a vocabulary of their language. Years later, all their words were discovered to form a language that was pure African Mandingo.

British authorities repeatedly tried to convince Native Americans to return the slave fugitives they harbored in their villages. But here they collided with an Indian adoption system that welcomed new members and offered them full protection. When whites argued about the right of private property in owning people and insisted Africans were inferior beings, the Indians usually shrugged "no."

In treaty after treaty southern colonists made native nations promise to return fugitive slaves. In 1721, the Five Civilized Nations solemnly promised a governor of Virginia to deliver slaves, but nothing happened. The British complained bitterly on behalf of their slave owners, the chiefs apologized, and the ex-slaves became a part of Native American life.

When angry slavehunters decided to take matters into their own hands, they met fierce opposition. In 1750 Captain Tobias Fitch sent off a posse of five to retrieve a slave living in the Creek Nation. A Creek chief stood between them and the black man, cut their rope and threw it in a fire. Then he warned them his villagers had as many guns as they did. The posse returned empty-handed but happy to be alive.

African members of Indian Nations often played a vital part in armed resistance to whites. In 1727 Africans and Indians besieged Virginia frontier settlements. During the French and Indian War a British officer, warning about the two races, said "Their mixing is to be prevented as much as possible."

The Northern British Colonies

In the New England and Middle Colonies African slaves were less numerous and therefore considered less dangerous. But in their actions and laws whites in these colonies showed they feared nonwhites uniting against them.

In 1690 a Connecticut law forbad red or black people from walking beyond town limits without a pass. Ferrymen were warned not to take either race across rivers. Connecticut, Rhode Island, and Massachusetts had laws imposing a nine o'clock curfew on Africans and Native Americans. Other New England laws were aimed at nonwhites who broke streetlights, sold liquor, or met together at night, or were entertained by Europeans.

Some laws specifically sought to prevent insurrections. In 1773 New York's Common Council in Albany passed a curfew "to prevent Negro and Indian slaves from appearing in the streets after eight at night without a lantern with a lighted candle in it."

They could not remain in Boston Common after sunset and were not allowed to carry a cane or stick "or anything

This early Rhode Island school for Afro-Americans and Native Americans sought to bring European ways to both peoples.

else that could be fit for quarreling or fighting." Rhode
Island, with the largest African population in New England,
banned their outdoor social gatherings.

These laws may have complicated and slowed, but failed
to halt associations between the two dark races. So many
slaves fled to the Six Nations of the Iroquois Confederacy
that, in 1726, a governor of New York made the leading
chiefs promise to return all fugitives in their villages. They
gave their word. In 1764 Hurons also promised. The next
year Delawares promised. None ever returned a single slave.

There are many instances, however, when the two peoples
acted in concert and terrified New England colonists. In
1660 African and Native American raiders panicked Hart-
ford, Connecticut, residents with an armed night assault. In
1690 Isaac Morill, British, James Dole, African, and Joseph
Moody, Indian, were arrested in Newbury, Connecticut, for
a major conspiracy against the state. Morill admitted help-
ing foment a rebellion with the French that would arm
Africans so "that the English would be cut off." Morrill and
his confederates planned to lead a French and Indian force
from Canada that would "save none but the Indians and
Negroes."

These startling revelations sent many colonists to bed
each night frightened lest this combination of foes might
prevent the dawn. Half a century later, in 1738, Nantucket,
Rhode Island, residents uncovered an Indian plot to attack
their city at night and only spare Africans.

Near Ontario, British colonists worried about the activi-
ties on Chief Joseph Brant's Mohawk reservation. Although
Brant was loyal to British interests, he welcomed slave runaways to his nation and may have encouraged his Mohawks
to marry them.

During Chief Pontiac's uprising against the British, Brant
and his Mohawks stood solidly by their British allies. But
around Detroit, reported a white resident, "the Indians are
saving and caressing all the Negroes they take." He was very
worried lest this might "produce an insurrection."

With few Indians or Africans in the northern colonies,
there were fewer opportunities for the two peoples to meet

or plot. And there were fewer numbers of Black Indians compared to what had become common in Virginia and the southern colonies at this time. These factors, and the relatively mild treatment of slaves by masters outside the south, made slaves less willing to risk so much by fleeing or planning rebellions.

It was not uncommon for New England slaves to view Indians much as their masters did and to side with whites during Indian warfare. In 1746 Lucy Terry, sixteen and African-born, witnessed a battle between Indians and her white neighbors in Deerfield, Massachusetts. Her rhymed story of it, "The Bar's Fight," described whites as valiant, brave, and bold and called Indians heartless murderers.

This poem became the first published by an African in the New World and made Terry a local celebrity, much in demand to recite her verses before local audiences.

From that point, Lucy Terry had no trouble with Native Americans. The same cannot be said about her relations with her white neighbors. She married an ex-slave, Elijah Prince, and two of their sons served in George Washington's Army. But the Princes were not destined to enjoy "the rights of man" promised by the patriot victory. Their prosperous farm was hit by a series of fires set by a neighbor who wanted the land. Haystacks were set afire and fences torn down at night. Through her determined plea before the governor, Lucy Prince won a cease and desist order.

When Mrs. Prince tried to enroll her youngest son in Williams College, she was told blacks were not welcome. She argued eloquently with the trustees, pointing to her family's military record, citing the Bible and the Declaration of Independence, but to no avail. When she died at ninety-one, in 1821, the Massachusetts legislature had established a committee to determine if the state could expel any black person who entered.

Perhaps the Lucy Terry Prince experience meant that a black person had less to fear from an Indian on the warpath than from a white man with a pen or plow.

By the end of the colonial period in British America, bondage had been confined to Africans, their children, and those Black Indians caught in the European web. Each century, great Native American figures arose to call on Indians of every nation to combine against the European invaders. There was King Philip in the 1670s, Pontiac in the 1760s, and Tecumseh in the 1810s. None understood that their best potential allies slept each night within a stone's throw of the enemy.

9

LIKE THE INDIANS THEMSELVES

Grizzled, uncouth, and unwashed, the old fur trappers looked more like the mountain bears they claimed they could wrestle than like men. They earned their place in history and talked their way into American folklore, and for good reason. They spun the tallest tales, especially to exaggerate their strength and accomplishments. But they also discovered more U.S. rivers and mountain passes than all the government expeditions sent out for that purpose.

But most incredibly, they rolled up this astounding record while seeking furs and pelts from Indians who sold them and hacking their way back to their customers in civilization.

Each day these frontiersmen faced mysterious perils. A snap of a twig, a screech from an unfamiliar bird, or the snarl of a ferocious animal might announce a brush with death. Sometimes there was no announcement. Trappers had to train eyes, ears, and nose to detect friend or foe— and to speedily note the difference.

Their business drove them ever westward, seeking remote Indians less likely to know the great value Europeans
placed on furs or skins. By 1850 their frontier daring had
taken simple hunting and transformed it into a major U.S.
industry.

The fur industry's business methods left a lot to be desired. General Zachary Taylor once characterized agents of
John Jacob Astor's huge American Fur Company as "the
greatest scoundrels the world ever knew."

Hollywood has stereotyped the fur trappers as men from
either Scotland or France. With names like McBayne or
Roget, Beaufont or MacIntosh—and accents to match the
names—white trappers strode across our silver screens.
None ever looked like Edward Rose, James Beckwourth,
or George and Pierre Bonga.

In reality, however, Afro-Americans were among the
trade's leading figures—as entrepreneurs, voyageurs, and
hunters. Colonel James Stevenson of the Bureau of American Ethnology spent thirty years living among and studying
Native Americans. In 1888 he wrote: ". . . the old fur
traders always got a Negro if possible to negotiate for them
with the Indians, because of their "pacifying effect." They
could manage them better than the white men, with less
friction."

Trading with Indians mixed diplomacy with business, and
that Native Americans preferred blacks to Europeans is
hardly surprising given the European record as conqueror.

Beginning in 1673, when fur trader Louis Joliet and
Father Jacques Marquette and five African and European
voyageurs paddled their canoes down the Mississippi to the
mouth of the Arkansas, black men were a vital part of fur-
trapping expeditions.

There is a problem in reconstructing the lives of black
trappers because white scholars have doubted their honesty.
The tall tale has always been a part of frontier Americana,
but black frontiersmen have been accused of so distorting
their personal stories as to blot out the truth.

James Beckwourth, for example, has long been considered, in the words of one professor, "rather as a great liar
than as a great 'mountain man.'" In 1848 General William

Tecumseh Sherman met Beckwourth and wrote this contra-
dictory judgment: "Jim Beckwourth . . . was in my estimate,
one of the best chroniclers of events on the plains that I
have ever encountered, though his reputation for veracity
was not good." For two pages of his book the famous
General described how a Beckwourth story, though doubted,
led to the capture of four murderers sought by the U.S.
Army.

Some frontier historians have admitted linking truthful-
ness to race. Historian Frances Parkman scribbled in his
personal copy of Beckwourth's autobiography "Much of
this narrative is probably false" and added "Beckwourth
is a fellow of bad character—a compound of white and
black blood." A more modern scholar has written that black
frontiersman Edward Rose was "a morose, moody misfit of
mixed blood and lawless disposition." Once blood is made
the measure of a person, it is the one who measures, not the
historical figure, who spins the distortion.

The factual evidence on Rose and Beckwourth shows
that they commanded high wages, were much in demand by
fur companies, and trusted by Native Americans. Frontier
businessmen or Native Americans were not likely to heap
rewards on chronic liars or men who could not be trusted
with valuables or other humans.

Edward Rose

The big news brought back by the Lewis and Clark expedition was that the huge Louisiana Territory was filled with
valuable fur animals and friendly Indians. The Missouri
River offered an all-water route to these rich hunting
grounds.

Of the fur-trading expeditions assembling in the winter of
1806–1807 at St. Louis, Manuel Lisa's proved the most
important. Into its ranks stepped Edward Rose, until that
moment a man of mystery and unknown accomplishments.
Perhaps he was too young or inexperienced to have
achieved a record at this date. Not even that is known.

The Lisa foray into the wilderness would forever establish Rose's reputation as one of the North American conti-

nent's leading frontiersmen, one sensitive to the task of dealing with Native Americans. The Lisa band sailed up the Missouri and Yellowstone rivers by keelboat and then built Fort Manuel at the mouth of the Big Horn. The men spent the next year's winter trapping, trading with natives, and fanning out from their camps to find more and more furs.

The Manuel Lisa expedition returned with the valuable news that greatest profits would go to large companies rather than individual traders. This information transformed the fur trade from a small operation into a company effort and a big business. Rose became one of the experts able to explain the best ways to operate in the wilderness.

He soon became a guide, hunter, and interpreter for the Missouri Fur Company, the Rocky Mountain Fur Company of William Ashley, and the American Fur Company of John Jacob Astor. Rose established a tradition of friendship between his white friends and the Native Americans they encountered.

His contemporaries described Rose as awesome. Thickset, muscular, above average in height, he had a slash on his nose, a scar on his forehead, and a grim, serious look. He meant business. No one knew if his slashed nose was a result of a fight or an accident; Indians called him "Cut-Nose." Rose came from ancestors that included Cherokees, Africans, and Europeans. He spoke a dozen Native American languages and Indian sign language.

Those who knew him well described Rose as strong, daring, and sometimes reckless, a man whose exploits matched anything in fiction. Washington Irving wrote of Rose in his *Astoria* and in the *Adventures of Captain Bonneville*, calling him "powerful in frame and fearless in spirit." Another author said Rose's "incredible career makes the most adventurous fiction seem weak and pallid."

Rose was ever on the move and always found his skills in demand. In 1809, he ventured with Ezekial Williams to the Yellowstone, the first land expedition into its beaver country. During the journey Rose proved capable of the sensitive task of guarding Mandan Chief Big White all the way back to his home. In 1811 Rose served as interpreter and guide for Wilson B. Hunt when he led Astor's men to western lands. The next year Rose was paid $250 for a one month trip of five hundred miles to the Crow Nation. When measured against the $250 yearly wage paid other trappers at the time, his pay was very high.

Rose, who became a Crow chief at one point in his career, built a solid reputation on his ability to handle Indians. He lived among various Native Americans for years, understood their languages and developed trusting relationships. This came in handy at least once. According to one report, when General Ashley's party was attacked by Native Americans, some of the attackers called out to Rose "to take care of himself, before they fired on General Ashley's party."

What exactly did he do to get along with Native Americans so well? In his 1848 book, *Five Scalps*, Captain Reuben Holmes describes Rose's qualities "that gained him the respect of the Indians" in these words:

> He was as cunning as a prairie wolf. He was a perfect woodsman. He could endure any kind of fatigue and privation as well as the best trained Indians. He studied men. There was nothing that an Indian could do, that Rose did not make himself master of. He knew all that Indians knew. He was a great man in his situation.

Rose, as much as Beckwourth and most trappers and frontiersmen, loved and told a good tale. It mixed fact with that personal brand of self-puffery known as the tall story. A recognized, imitated, and enjoyable form of frontier humor, it began with Captain John Smith and Daniel Boone and still rides high with hunters and fishermen.

Rose and Beckwourth did expand a truth when it touched on their skills and accomplishments. They also let the flow of events and the efforts of others to go on undisturbed.

George and Stephen Bonga

Compared with the explosive life of Edward Rose, the calm, businesslike fur-trapping experiences of the Bonga brothers seem as quiet as a frozen Minnesota lake. However, this frontier Black Chippewa family negotiated some key Indian treaties for the U.S. government and built some important Minnesota trading outposts.

The first Bongas to arrive in Minnesota were a slave couple brought there by a British officer after the American Revolution. They had a son Pierre, who was apprenticed to a Canadian trapper for the North West Company and was well trusted. Together with a white man, he was put in charge of the company fort when his master left on business. In time Pierre Bonga became an interpreter for the North West Company. While negotiating in a Chippewa village he met and fell in love with a Chippewa woman, and they were married.

Pierre Bonga and his bride settled in Duluth half a century before a permanent European settlement was established there. During the presidency of Thomas Jefferson their son George was born, and his father was able to send him to school in Montreal. When he returned home, George also chose a Chippewa woman as his bride. George and his brother Stephen followed in their father's footsteps, becoming fur trappers, learning French and English, Chippewa, and other Indian languages.

George Bonga cultivated a close relationship with the twenty-five thousand-strong Chippewa Nation at a critical time for the U.S. government. In 1837, at Fort Snelling, George Bonga was able to negotiate a key treaty between his country and his people for Governor Lewis Cass of the Michigan Territory. Cass later became a presidential candidate who liked to tell of his part in this historic transaction.

In his work as a trapper, George Bonga served as a voyageur for the American Fur Company, maintaining posts at La Platte, Otter Tail Lake, and Leech Lake, where he made his home.

The Bonga brothers were tall, powerfully built, ebony-black men. They were known in Minnesota for their gentle ways, quick humor, love of storytelling, and hospitality.

In 1856, as the slavery controversy exploded into border warfare in Kansas, George Bonga and his wife entertained a distinguished guest. Judge Charles Flandreau, after an exhausting canoe trip to the source of the Mississippi, came to their cabin and was invited to stay for two weeks.

George Bonga, whom Flandreau described as "the blackest man I ever saw," regaled his guests with tales of old trapping experiences. Everyone enjoyed a laugh when Bonga said, "Gentlemen, I assure you that John Banfil and myself were the first two white men that ever came to this country."

To amuse his guest, Bonga assembled a crew for an early-days lake voyage, complete with "a splendid birch bark canoe," manned by twelve hearty men. Led by Bonga and "to the music of a French Canadian," the judge learned "how royally they travelled" when Minnesota was a wild country.

Some forty-two years later, then associate justice of the Minnesota Supreme Court, Flandreau wrote of his vacation with "this thorough gentleman" and "prominent trader and man of wealth and consequence." It is the only account that exists of George Bonga's personal side.

The next year the Bongas entertained two traders at their Otter Tail Lake post. This time the Black Chippewa eagerly asked "about elections and political matters." The U.S. was hurtling toward Civil War and black people had a vital stake in the day's political questions.

The Bonga family bequeathed the state of Minnesota about a hundred descendants and gave their name to Bonga township in Cass County.

James P. Beckwourth

Black trappers tried mightily to build bridges of understanding with Native Americans, sometimes cemented with the bonds of marriage. James Beckwourth also married Indian women, sometimes in dizzyingly rapid succession. But with his flaming temper and love of battle he kept burning his bridges down.

Beckwourth became a chieftain of both Crow and Blackfoot Indian Nations, so he enjoyed many supporters and

George Bonga followed in his father's footsteps, marrying a Chippewa and becoming a noted fur trapper.

admirers. Beckwourth also emerges from the fur trade's early history as "the greatest Indian fighter of his generation." This was an age when his competitors for this "honor" were Daniel Boone, Davy Crockett, Jim Bridger, and Kit Carson.

It is difficult to imagine that this famed frontiersman, scout, and explorer has faded from the story of the Old West, but fade he did. In skill, accomplishment, and violence, he matched men whose deeds have become part of a glorious frontier heritage. But when Universal International in Hollywood produced the horse opera *Tomahawk*, it cast white actor Jack Oakie as Jim Beckwourth. Generations of young people never learned that this tough pioneer fur trapper was a black man.

In the 1951 movie Tomahawk, *Jack Oakie (left) played Jim Beckwourth so audiences never learned his race.*

Beckwourth was born around 1798 to a black slave and her white master. As a teen-ager, he was apprenticed to a St. Louis blacksmith. His western adventures began with a punch. When the burly blacksmith came between Beckwourth and his liberty at nineteen to come and go as he pleased, Beckwourth slugged him and left St. Louis for the wilderness. Though hardly original, he had "hit" upon the solution to problems he would use from there on.

In a business that moved as fast as foot, boat, or horse could carry it, Beckwourth swept from one end of the continent to the other, from St. Louis to Salt Lake, from California to Florida, from New Orleans to Nevada. On the trail he fought or made friends with Native American Blackfeet, Sac, Snakes, and Crows.

His Indian wives invariably were royalty, daughters of

chiefs who could do Beckwourth some good. No woman ever held him for very long, and one Blackfoot chief's daughter was almost killed by Beckwourth on his wedding night. When she refused to obey his command not to dance, he clobbered her with the side of an axe. Turning to her father, he explained that discipline had to be maintained by the husband.

The chief not only agreed, but gave him a new daughter. That night Beckwourth and his second wife of the day were spending their honeymoon in a teepee when the first wife came crawling back. Beckwourth settled the matter by giving both women presents and then taking his leave.

In a Crow village, Beckwourth was adopted into the nation and married the chief's daughter. First named "Morning Star," after leading Crows into battle, he was renamed "Bloody Arm." He soon found life among the Crows too quiet and left for new excitement.

In the 1830s he served as a U.S. Army scout in the Seminole wars—against the Black Seminole alliance in Florida. Enemies were enemies and a good fight, after all, was a good fight. In 1843 Pathfinder John C. Frémont met Beckwourth traveling with a Spanish wife sixty miles east of the Rockies. Another time Beckworth met General Kearny during California's Bear Flag Rebellion. Kearny told him "You like war, and I have good use for you now."

Later Beckwourth prospected for gold, trapped some more, and wandered. By then he carried such Indian names as Bull's Robe, Medicine Calf, and White-Handled Knife. He dressed, looked, and acted like a Native American. When he became a Crow chief, he led his men into battle stripped down and shouting, "I will show you how to fight."

In April 1850, Beckwourth made a discovery that should have forever earned him a place in U.S. history books. Northwest of what is now Reno, Nevada, and on what is now Route 70 in California, he found a pass through the Sierra Nevada mountains. It soon became an important gateway to Gold Rush California.

Today the pass, mountain peak, and town nearby still bear Beckwourth's name. He personally led the first wagon

Frontiersman James P. Beckwourth led the Crow Nation soon after he married the daughter of the Crow ruler.

train through Beckwourth Pass. Later he built a hotel and retired to become a peaceful innkeeper.

In 1855 Beckwourth met journalist T. D. Bonner in San Francisco and the two began to collaborate on *The Life and Adventures of James P. Beckwourth*. Beckwourth talked and Bonner wrote and the resulting volume appeared the next year. It is silent on the matter of Beckwourth's dark ancestors, and its artist's sketches make him appear white.

In 1866 Beckwourth died of food poisoning while traveling to or from a Crow village. This simple fact has given rise to a legend: He was invited back to his Crow people by those who hoped he would consent to lead them again. When Beckwourth refused, this legend continues, he was given a feast and poisoned. Unable to have him as a live chief, Crows would keep him forever in their burial grounds. This fantasy touches truth in the admiration his fellow Crows had for him, and in their profound sense of loss when he picked up and left them.

Beckwourth was part of that daring, brutal frontier tradition that opened the wilderness to exploration and settlement. Here was clearly a man suited to the dangers of the trail, one who fought and killed with ease and even pleasure. "Probably no man ever lived who has met with more personal adventure including danger to life," wrote his biographer, T. D. Bonner.

Even if this is an exaggeration, it indicates that Beckwourth belongs in the pages of our violent frontier epic as much as his better known white contemporaries.

10

BLOOD SO LARGELY MINGLED

In the decades before the Civil War, frantic slaveholders tried to nail down and secure their leaky system. For seven cents an hour they hired armed patrols to scour the countryside every night. Savage beatings awaited any black man, woman, or child walking without a pass. Runaways were tracked with savage dogs. Free blacks were carefully watched lest they give aid and comfort to fleeing sisters and brothers—which they often did. Even antislavery whites were warned, tarred and feathered, or driven from their homes.

But there was one slave escape hatch that drove slaveowners to sputtering fury. Whites looked at Native American villages in the South and found black faces staring back at them. Paranoia told whites that these people were about to rise up, liberate slaves, and kill whites.

This haunting Black Indian presence spelled a trouble or

doom that had to be dealt with. One hysterical response was to demand that state legislatures remove Indians from tax exempt lands, and then drive them away.

In 1843, for example, white residents of King William County, Virginia, felt their world was coming to an end— "unhinged" they said. As a slaveholding community they petitioned their legislature to save them from what they termed a "dangerous" and "deadly" peril. At any moment they anticipated an attack by land and sea.

Their great fear was prompted by a peaceful community of Pamunkey Indians, many of whom were biracial or free black men and women. Rather than expose their dangerous actions or suspected conspiracies, whites just kept pointing to the fact they were Black Indians. "Not one individual can be found among them whose grandfathers or grand-mothers one or more is not of Negro blood," read the white petition to the legislature.

The other white complaint charged these Pamunkeys had allowed their land to become a "resort of free Negroes from all parts of the country" and a "harbour for runaway slaves." No evidence was offered for either accusation. But whites asked Virginia's assembly to deny the Pamunkeys their tax exemption and investigate their subversion of Virginia.

The real meaning of this furor was that it had become clear to any who cared to look that Native Americans east of the Mississippi had become a biracial people (with a sprinkling of white blood). In slaveholding regions this prompted white panic, and in northern states it led to legislative investigations.

Along the Atlantic Coast

Slaveholders knew better than anyone that almost anything might disrupt their slave system. The presence of Indian communities on their borders that included blacks spelled possible sabotage, subversion, and a haven for slave runaways.

Petitions against the Gingaskin reservation began to

Opposite page:
*From the Atlantic to the Pacific and Gulf of Mexico, two dark races
met and married.*

reach the Virginia legislature as early as 1783. Whites in
Northampton County complained free blacks and "other
disorderly persons" were hiding there. When this petition
failed, they tried again three years later, and lost again.

They petitioned again in 1812. This time war fever was
loose in the land, and in Florida armed Seminoles openly
defied U.S. troops and slavehunters. The Virginia legislature removed the Gingaskins' tax exemption, saying they
were no longer "Indians."

The Melungeon Indians in Tennessee and North Carolina
faced similar charges. Whites in Tennessee declared Melungeons "free persons of color," so they continued to accept
and marry black people. But in 1855, North Carolina
Melungeons were forbidden to marry black people. The
state legislature decided that these Melungeons were really
Croatans. Croatans were considered white descendants of
Sir Walter Raleigh's lost English colony of Roanoke. The
Melungeon's "race" shifted with white legal decisions in
their home states.

In the decades between the American Revolution and
the Civil War Black Indian societies were reported in New
Jersey, New York, Delaware, Maryland, Virginia, North
Carolina, South Carolina, Connecticut, Tennessee, and
Massachusetts. Some managed to live as maroons, distant
from a white society they rejected.

White citizens viewed these communities with feelings
ranging from curiosity to suspicion and dread. White
citizens charged some with being dangerous to or a stain
on the larger society. Others were accused of dangerous
inbreeding. White men kept their wives and children away,
and kept their powder dry and ready for battle.

Northern states were also concerned enough by a Black
Indian presence to send investigators. Rhode Island, Long
Island, and New Jersey reported thorough mixtures of the
two peoples. A report on the Narragansetts found they were

"nearly all . . . of mixed blood and color, in various degrees
and shades." The same was said in state reports on New
York's Southhampton and Montauk Indians. A shocked
legislature concluded "they are only Indian in name." New
Jersey state investigators claimed their Native Americans
had lost their "Indian features."

Nowhere was the blending of Native American and
African people clearer than in Massachusetts. Pioneer black
historian Carter G. Woodson discovered an 1861 report
by the state senate that listed Black Indians among most
Massachusetts Indians: Hassanamisco, Middleborough,
Chappequiddick, Christiantown, Gay Head, Marshpee,
Herring Pond, Fall River, and Dudley. Turning from these
files to interview people in 1919, Woodson found black
residents who could trace their ancestry back to the famous
Massasoit.

Wildfire, or Edmonia Lewis

Perhaps the most artistically talented Black Indian of these
eastern Nations was Wildfire or Edmonia Lewis, daughter
of a Chippewa mother and a black father. Only three when
her mother died in 1849, she was left in the care of two
Chippewa aunts. She grew up in upstate New York making
and selling moccasins, bead baskets, and pincushions.
"Until I was twelve years old," she recalled, "I led this
wandering life, fishing and swimming." During this time
she was known by her Chippewa name of Wildfire.

From 1860 to 1862, with funds supplied by her brother,
Sunrise, she attended Oberlin College. There she changed
her name to Edmonia Lewis and began to show an interest
in sculpture. In a terrifying turn of events, she was accused
and tried for poisoning two white Oberlin friends. In a well-
publicized trial, she won an acquittal. Even this bizarre
intrusion did not keep her from pursuing her artistic interest.
She did have a "thought of returning to the wild life again,
but my love of sculpture forbade it."

Lewis left Oberlin for Boston, where she met prominent
black and white abolitionists and established her first studio.

"I had always wanted to make the forms of things, and while I was at school I tried to make drawings of people and things." She recalled that her mother had invented artistic patterns for embroidery and "perhaps the same thing is coming out in me in a more civilized form."

In 1864, while attending an antislavery meeting, Edmonia Lewis was interviewed by the noted children's writer, Lydia Maria Child. Mrs. Child quoted Lewis on her Indian background:

> No, I have not a single drop of what is called white blood in my veins. My father was a full-blooded Negro, and my mother was a full-blooded Chippewa. . . .
> And have you lived with the Chippewas?
> Yes. When my mother was dying, she wanted me to promise that I would live three years with her people, and I did.
> And what did you do while you were there?
> I did as my mother's people did. I made baskets and embroidered moccasins and I went into the cities with my mother's people to sell them. . . .

Lewis then showed Mrs. Child a bust of Voltaire she was completing, and offered this comment: "I don't want you to go to praise me," she said, "for I know praise is not good for me. Some praise me because I am a colored girl, and I don't want that kind of praise. I had rather you would point out my defects, for that will teach me something."

During her long artistic career in the United States and Europe, Edmonia Lewis asked for and benefited from criticism. Shortly after this interview she left for Europe and established a studio in Rome. She turned out portrait busts of her heroes: Abraham Lincoln; abolitionists Charles Sumner, William L. Garrison, and Maria Chapman; and her favorite white figure, John Brown.

In 1876 her *Death of Cleopatra* was first exhibited at the Philadelphia Centennial Exposition and drew critical praise as "the grandest statue in the exposition." It weighed over two tons, stood twelve feet tall, and took over four years to make. By this time the works of Edmonia Lewis were ex-

Edmonia Lewis followed in her mother's footsteps.

hibited and sold from New York and Boston to Minnesota and California, and in Europe.

Her works were commissioned by wealthy patrons, and she became a celebrity whose Rome studio drew tourists and the curious. She was considered an eccentric by some who commented about her "masculine look," careless dress style, and "personal peculiarities."

Edmonia Lewis was a short woman with straight black, abundant hair and "a proud spirit," which she believed came from her mother. She was known for her honest talk about her early hard times.

Visitors to her Rome studio remembered she had a tendency to lapse into "quietude and stoicism." Others recalled a demeanor that showed the "sadness of African and Indian races."

The date and place of her death are not known.

Texas and California before the Civil War

Plains Indian Nations—the Commanches, Kiowas, Lipans, and Apaches—became tough, hard-riding people who challenged the European invader on countless battlefields.

They had no slaves and saw foreigners of any color or language as a danger. For them Africans brought West by white masters were part of an enemy advance on their civilization. Slave and master were part of the same tide that would swallow up Native American life on the Great Plains and the deserts of the southwest. Both white and black dressed like Europeans, used the same tools, and lived in houses.

Many slaves, picked for their loyalty before being brought to the wilderness, stood by their masters on the frontier. But despite a master's careful selection, some slaves bolted for freedom at the earliest opportunity.

During Texas's Lone Star Rebellion, Colonel James Morgan reported black slaves were seeking contacts with Texas Indians, and "wished to join the Mexicans," so they could be free. The next year a Mexican General led Biloxi Indians, Mexicans, and blacks against U.S. whites. In one battle two blacks died and one, a large man who spoke French, was captured. He defiantly shouted he had always been free and had no respect for the Texas government. A firing squad promptly shot him.

Luckier was a black man married to an Indian and living in her village near Carson City, Nevada, in 1860. He was caught running guns, ammunition, and bowie knives to nearby Indians. He admitted to his captors he had been doing it for years and that he had a Quaker partner. Before he was punished, he managed to escape. His Quaker partner was not found.

In California Africans constituted a significant part of the population under Spanish rule and mixed easily with Native Americans. A Spanish census of 1790 found 18 percent of the population of San Francisco, 24 percent of San Jose, 20 percent of Santa Barbara, and 18 percent of Monterey had black ancestors.

The city of Los Angeles was founded in 1781 by forty-four people, of whom only two were Europeans, and the rest African, Indian, or a mixture of the three races. Maria Rita Valdez, a granddaughter of one black founder, owned a section of land we call Beverly Hills today. Francisco Reyes, another founder, owned the San Fernando Valley.

This antique French print preserves some Black Indians found in Spanish California before the U.S. arrival.

In the 1790s he sold it and became mayor of Los Angeles.

The governor of California before the arrival of the U.S. armed forced was Pio Pico. Governor Pico came from a prominent California family with African ancestors.

The arrival of U.S. rule changed life in California. Under Spain and Mexico about 15 percent of Californians had listed themselves as African in heritage. This population disappeared on U.S. Census rolls. Slavery, racial animosity, and California's new "Black Laws" drove them across to the safe side of the invisible color line.

Little is known about the Black Indians who strode or rode across California's trails after that. One white pioneer remembered a black man preaching to Native Americans in their own language near the Canadian River. He also reported that on the Santa Fe trail black people "have a great deal of influence with the Indians." At Fort Kearny he found a black interpreter using his knowledge of Spanish and Indian languages to provide U.S. authorities with valuable information.

Slavery in the Five Civilized Nations

The Choctaw, Chickasaw, Cherokee, Creek, and Seminole Nations were early penetrated by European merchants, missionaries, and government officials. Because they readily accepted Christianity, and European styles in houses and dress, whites began to call them "The Five Civilized Tribes." With the notable exception of the Seminoles, some members also became slaveowners.

Since these nations lived on thousands of acres in the heart of the South, their acceptance of bondage was considered vital. Indian slaveholders would no longer accept runaways, because they understood the value of slave labor. In short, a major escape route and potential set of allies had dried up for millions of Africans held in chains.

By 1860 slavery had become a major part of life for the Four Civilized Nations. Only the Seminoles, as we have already seen, firmly rejected bondage in favor of a system of friendship and alliance with their black members. But among the other Four Nations black slavery began to shape their development and village life.

It divided each nation into a wealthy slaveholding minority and a poorer majority. For example, among Cherokees only 12 percent owned slaves. Slaves made up 18 percent of the Cherokees, 14 percent of the Choctaws, 18 percent of the Chickasaws, and 10 percent of the Creeks.

Slavery pushed Native Americans into some crucial economic and cultural changes. Before skill and character had counted, but now race became important in judging people. The Cherokees and others adopted "Slave Codes" to control their black men and women, prevent their escape and even their learning to read and write. If a slave ran off or rebelled, Indian Slave Codes required other members of the nation to help catch him or her.

Slavery also altered the basic economies of these nations. Each turned from hunting and fishing to tilling huge plantations with slave labor. This labor surplus produced enough crops to sell in the open market. Slavery had driven four major Indian Nations into an era of capitalist expansion and labor exploitation.

Bondage is always a violation of the human spirit and the will to be free. But most observers found that the chains of slavery were fitted rather loosely on black people owned by Indians. Only the Chickasaws had a reputation for treating their slaves as badly as did white masters. The other nations practiced such a mild form of bondage that it upset U.S. slave owners. The Seminoles, of course, infuriated white and Indian masters with their generosity, fairness, and a level of equality toward their "slaves."

What was bondage like for those held by Native Americans? In interviews conducted during the 1930s, former slaves evaluated their experiences differently. Johnson Thompson, eighty, and a former Cherokee slave, said: "The master never punish anybody, and I never see anybody whipped, and only one slave sold. Lots of slave children didn't ever learn to read."

Rochelle Ward, ninety-one, remembered: "Some of the slaves work around and get money and pay this money to their master for freedom, so there was some freed before the close of the war. Some of the others tried to run away after the war started."

Chaney Rickardson, ninety, recalled: "None of the Cherokees ever whipped us, and my mistress gave me some mighty fine rules to live by. Didn't have no jails for Negroes and no jail for themselves. We all had plenty to eat."

Whites who visited slaveholding Indians described slave men and women who were well-treated, adequately fed and cared for. U.S. slaveholders viewed this leniency as a sign Native Americans did not understand bondage. They also thought it posed a danger to their own ability to control their black laborers. If Native Americans did not know how to treat slaves, then something would have to be done about Native Americans.

The Trail of Tears

For white U.S. citizens in the eastern states problems presented by Native Americans were solved in a single dramatic stroke by the Indian Removal Act of 1830. It provided for the mass deportation of the Five Civilized Nations from their huge, fertile homelands in the southeast.

Some sixty thousand red and black men and women were eventually deposited on lands in Arkansas and Oklahoma that whites considered uninhabitable. In 1832 the Choctaws were driven westward to this new "Indian Territory" in midwinter. They were among the first to leave blood-stained footsteps in the snow.

Removal meant more than a change of geography. Fragile cultures were uprooted by Army troops and driven to an alien climate and location.

For Cherokees it was a murderous "trail of tears." President Martin Van Buren ordered seven thousand soldiers under General Winfield Scott to move a nation of fourteen thousand. Homes were burned, livestock, tools, printing presses, and personal possessions seized and destroyed.

Cherokee men, women, and children, including one thousand six hundred Black Cherokees were prodded westward in midwinter by Federal bayonets. About ten thousand Cherokees survived, but President Van Buren assured Congress that their expulsion "had the happiest effects. . . . The Cherokees have emigrated without apparent reluctance."

In the Indian Territory the Civilized Nations, decimated by their deadly journey, faced a wilderness. Clearing was necessary before settlements could survive. Those who had left their dead on the long trail across the South to the Mississippi and beyond now had to turn to building new homes. Only a rich cultural heritage and strong families provided the fortitude necessary to sustain nations.

On their new lands Indians faced new assaults. Whites seeking to profit from their misery appeared in their camps with products to sell. Native Americans became even more dependent upon white goods and values. Government "Indian agents" regulated their lives and paved the way for other intruders. Slavery became even more entrenched.

The Indian agents sent by Washington openly encouraged slaveholding. Soon two distinct classes based on slave ownership divided each Indian Nation. "Mixed bloods" owned slaves and usually had some white ancestry. Though a minority, they felt both of these facts made them superior, fit to rule. This also meant the amount of "white" blood was a positive, much as the amount of "black" blood was a negative. "Full bloods" formed a majority, but because they had no white blood and held no slaves, they had little power.

Between 1830 and 1860 the population of the Four Nations declined sharply, Cherokees by 31 percent, Choctaws by 27 percent, Chickasaws by 18 percent, and Creeks by 43 percent. At the same time the number of members with white blood increased and so too did the number of slaves each nation held. By 1860 Cherokees had 2,511 slaves, Choctaws 2,344, Creeks 1,532, and Chickasaws 975.

Slavery had become the major economic and political factor in these nations. This meant that their racial thinking was approaching that of the white South.

However, visitors to the Indian Territory reported an Indian type of bondage that hardly matched the harshness and cruelty of whites.

In 1853 German artist Möllhausen wrote:

These slaves receive from the Indian masters more Christian treatment than among the Christian whites. The traveler may seek in vain for any other difference between master and servant than such as nature has made in the physical characteristics of the races; and the Negro is regarded as a companion and helper, to whom thanks and kindness are due when he exerts himself for the welfare of the household.

The mild bondage practiced by Indians soon came under sharp attack by neighboring white slaveholders and U.S. Indian agents. Choctaw Agent Douglas Cooper thought that Choctaws, Cherokees, and Creeks should have white U.S. owners of slaves live in their villages and "control matters." (The Chickasaws, it will be remembered, were considered almost as harsh as white masters.)

Elias Rector, Superintendent of Southern Indian Affairs in 1859, had another thought. He suggested that every Indian family should own slaves because it would tend "to civilize them." He also believed Indians would benefit from

This group of Sac Fox Native Americans includes at least one Afro-American.

black slaves "who could teach them to cultivate the soil and properly prepare and cook their foods."

Though whites became upset at the leniency of Indian slavery, slaves themselves reached a different conclusion. At four in the morning, on November 15, 1842, black men and women on Cherokee land owned by the Vann family near Weber Falls mutinied. Creek and Cherokee slaves locked overseers in cabins, seized guns, horses, and provisions and then gathered up their children for a dash to Mexico. Black Seminoles were suspected of having sparked the rebellion.

An estimated 60 to 250 slaves joined a liberation march singing "I'll tell you, Marsa Ben, your Niggers gwine to leave you!" Armed Cherokees mounted up and rode after them, but were defeated in a two-day battle. Finally, fresh Cherokee troops arrived to overwhelm the rebels on an open prairie. The survivors were brought back, some to be executed, others whipped.

That same year hunters on the Washita River reported a fort garrisoned by one to two hundred runaway slaves from the Indian Territory. For the next eighteen years whites believed "outlaw negroes" were responsible for murders along the Choctaw border.

To the extent that some Native Americans adopted a mean-spirited, profit-hungry slavery urged on them by whites and Indian agents, they faced the same rebelliousness that marked the southern states. But, despite the inducements and pressures, most rejected that foreign standard and followed their own gentler instincts. This simple decision stands as yet another example of a treasured independent spirit by Native Americans. The beneficiaries were the Afro-Americans whose slave years were spent with people who found it very difficult to treat other human beings as pieces of property.

11

THE FINEST SPECIMENS OF MANKIND

The Civil War pitted brother against brother, and nowhere more painfully than among the Five Civilized Nations. "Mixed bloods," committed to slavery clashed with "full bloods" and their black allies who just wanted to be left in peace.

The Indian Territory in 1861 was surrounded by the Confederacy and flooded with its agents and sympathizers. Then Confederate officials and troops arrived to control matters and U.S. power was nowhere in sight. By the time Fort Sumter surrendered that April, Chickasaws and Choctaws had signed treaties with the Confederacy. Cherokees, Creeks, and Seminoles were told by Confederate officials "there ain't no more U.S.—ain't any more Treaty—all be dead." By August the leaders of these nations had caved in and allied their members to the new Confederacy.

An Indian Civil War

Red and Black Indians favoring neutrality or the Union (including most black members) grouped around a wealthy Creek Chief, Opothle Yahola. He secretly wrote to President Lincoln asking for the protection promised, saying "now the wolf has come. Men who are strangers tread our soil. Our children are frightened & mothers cannot sleep for fear." Getting this letter to the Union forces proved almost impossible. Getting Union help in 1861 was impossible.

Opothle Yahola and his followers hoped to live out the war in peace. They moved away from the pro-Confederate Indians and camped out on the Indian Territory's southwestern frontier—men, women, and children with stores of food, livestock, and wagons of possessions. Half of the Seminole Nation joined them, as well as blacks from all Five Nations and Kickapoos, Shawnees, Delawares, and Commanches.

Confederate Creek soldiers wanted to attack the camp and seize Opothle Yahola as a traitor. Douglas Cooper, U.S. Indian agent, now serving as commander of Indian Confederate troops, restrained them.

Finally when Cooper's forces advanced on the camp with troops composed of Choctaws, Creeks, Chickasaws, and white Texas cavalry regiments, it was deserted. The "peace" Indians had picked up and left on a long trail. The Confederate forces assumed they were headed toward Union lines in Kansas. Actually they were circling around searching for other peace pro-Union Cherokees.

The week before Thanksgiving, Confederates tracked down the Opothle Yahola party near Stillwater and attacked. The peace forces regrouped and continued their march into the Cherokee Nation. Two weeks later Cooper's regiments, including fresh Cherokee troops, caught up with them. When the battle began these Cherokee soldiers deserted to the peace band.

This larger conglomeration of neutral Indians made their headquarters and built a stronghold north of Tulsa. The day after Christmas Confederate troops again attacked and desperate hand-to-hand fighting began.

The peace forces were defeated and fled, abandoning their wagons, bedding, and clothing. They lost about 900 cattle, 250 ponies, and 190 sheep and took off on foot through a blizzard toward Kansas and the Union lines. Desperate men tried to cover the retreat of their women and children with weapons they found. Said one Seminole chief "At that battle we lost everything we possessed, everything to take care of our women and children with, and all that we had. . . . We left them in cold blood by the wayside."

During the fighting and forced march many froze to death. Bodies were devoured by wolves.

After a long forced march, the survivors reached Kansas and had to camp without blankets on ground that was still frozen. Once he had been a rich man, owning many slaves and cattle, but now Apothle Yahola had lost his daughter on the daring march, and he was very ill. He died within a year, knowing he had led a bold exodus for freedom through the winter snows. By April, as the first buds of spring came through the soil, some 7,600 in his camp were receiving U.S. Army supplies and his men were talking of enlisting as Union soldiers.

One of the first regiments formed by these red and black men was led by Jim Lane, a flamboyant Kansas senator. Only five years earlier Lane publicly stated that the African was a connecting link between human and orangutan. After leading some Black Indians into battle he changed his tune. He now believed they were "the finest specimens of manhood I have ever gazed upon."

Freedom Comes to the Five Civilized Nations

The defeat of the Confederacy gave the U.S. government a new opportunity to impose its will on Native Americans, most of whom had become allies of the Confederacy. Existing treaties were scrapped. A large portion of Indian Territory was taken from the Five Nations by the Federal government and handed to the Plains Nations, Shawnees, and Delawares.

Emancipation also was imposed from outside. The U.S. government and white citizens had once demanded Native

This 1861 print shows swashbuckling Jim Lane, leader of red and black scouts for the Union army in Kansas.

Americans adopt slavery and hunt runaways. Now they demanded that all slaves of Indians become free and equal. The white man had again spoken with forked tongue and, as always, in his own interest.

Seminoles, whose blacks often had been dear friends and family members, quickly accepted emancipation and equality. Soon Cherokees and Creeks did. Choctaws resisted for a generation and Chickasaws fought the issue almost to the end of the century. Except for the Seminoles, within each nation black members faced years of legal challenges and political protests to win citizenship rights, land, education, and equality of opportunity. The black effort in the Indian Territory reflected their wider and less successful campaign for equality during this era of Reconstruction in the southern states.

Among the Seminoles, blacks were immediately liberated and six were elected to the forty-two-seat Seminole Council. By the end of freedom's first year Black Seminoles were building homes, churches, schools, and businesses, planting and harvesting crops. Parents showed an avid interest in education for their children, and some adults even attended night schools.

Black members of other Indian Nations worked vigorously for equality, land ownership, and education. Very few left their host nation. Whatever unfairness they felt among their Indian friends could not match what they would experience among whites. They knew this and stayed. Here were a people who would never lynch or brutalize their sons and daughters.

Among Creeks, Seminoles, and Cherokees, black people made economic strides they could rarely duplicate in U.S. society. Black Cherokees owned barbershops, blacksmith shops, general stores, and restaurants. Some had become printers, ferry-boat operators, cotton-gin managers, teachers, and postmasters.

As early as 1866, John B. Sanborn, Commissioner of Indian Affairs, reported from the Indian Territory:

> The freedmen are the most industrious, economical, and in many respects, the more intelligent portion of the population of the Indian Territory. They all desire to remain in that territory upon lands set apart for their own exclusive use.

Even as ex-slaves among Cherokees, Creeks, and Seminoles were making these rapid strides, those among the Choctaws and Chickasaws suffered. Black men who had fought for the Union during the Civil War found they and their families were denied full membership. Commissioner Sanborn found it was "not safe or advisable" for some former soldiers to even return to their villages. Conditions in these nations changed very slowly.

The black thirst for education that blossomed throughout the former slave states bloomed among the Civilized Nations as well. Collecting money from poor but interested parents, Black Indians built their own schools, hired and paid teachers, and then asked for additional government aid. An 1866 government report on Black Creeks revealed they "are anxious that their children shall be educated" and are "determined to profit" from "the school formed at their own advance."

The first choice of Black Indians was to have their children educated in the same classrooms as other members of their nation. But that desire often failed, and so they sought funds to begin their own schools. When even that failed, and often before, they converted homes and churches into schools.

This early Oklahoma school had red and black Indian students and teachers.

They were urged on by educated professionals among their members. O. S. Fox, editor of the Cherokee *Afro-American Advocate* wrote: "If you have to make a sacrifice make it and fill that school up. To be anything the Indian must be educated."

Arthur Bean wrote in his agreement: "By all means let us have some sort of school. I say that he is no man at all who cannot pay one dollar a month to have his children educated."

Slowly but surely, the Five Civilized Nations, even the resistant Chickasaws, agreed to provide financial support for Black Indian schools. By 1907 Chickasaws operated twenty-one schools for black members, and some were integrated.

The Black Indian campaign for full citizenship was carried on with forceful but respectful language. In 1879 a group of Black Cherokees petitioned for equal rights:

> The Cherokee nation is our country; there we were born and reared; there are our homes made by the sweat of our brows; there are our wives and children, whom we love as dearly as though we were born with red, instead of black skins. There we intend to live and defend our natural rights, as guaranteed by the treaties and laws of the United States, by every legitimate and lawful means.

Even as they pressured and demanded, O. S. Fox reminded his fellow Black Indians of the benefits of remaining among their red friends:

> The opportunities for our people in that country far surpassed any of the kind possessed by our people in the U.S. . . . It is nonsense for any Afro-American to emigrate to Africa or anywhere else if he can make a living in the Indian Territory.

In 1884, as the Chickasaw Nation argued the merits of granting equality to black members, a convention of Black Chickasaws met and affirmed their loyalty to the nation:

> As natives, we are attached to the people among whom we have been born and bred. We like the Chickasaws as

friends and we know by the experience of the past that we
can live with them in the future in a close union. . . .

At the end of the Civil War and for a variety of reasons,
many Afro-Americans left white society to enter Indian
Nations. Thousands stayed to marry Indian women or men,
raise children, and make their living in an accepting culture
that was not burdened down with hatreds based on skin
color. Since so many remained, it can be assumed that they
found a greater fulfillment there than elsewhere.

During this time many white people also joined Indian
Nations. Some people of both races were probably attracted
by the cash or land offerings the U.S. government made to
settle accounts with Native Americans. But beyond these
self-seekers were many who concluded that Native Americans understood freedom, family, and law better than the
surrounding white societies of the day.

From Territory to Statehood

U.S. citizens first became aware of good grasslands in the
Indian Territory during the great cattle drives that passed
through to Kansas after the Civil War. By 1872, the railroad had sent its iron horse chugging through Oklahoma's
fertile plains. Now there was no stopping land-hungry
pioneers. By the 1880s the U.S. government and its mounted
infantry and cavalry regiments formed a thin blue line of
protection against white intruders.

But there was no stemming this white lust for settlement.
A dream of land and an appetite for economic gain had
always powered the white pioneer spirit. It soon collided
with a Federal pledge to keep Native Americans safe on
these lands. A white "boomer" invasion began in 1880,
truculently crashing through to build camps, only to be
ejected by the U.S. Army. White and black soldiers, often
reluctantly, escorted boomers out each time.

The boomers grew to an estimated forty thousand, and
most swore an oath to keep fighting until Oklahoma was
theirs. By 1889, the government joined the movement and
forced both Creeks and Seminoles to surrender their land

rights in return for cash. An Oklahoma land rush was organized for U.S. citizens.

On April 22, 1889, an estimated one hundred thousand men, women, and children on horses, bicycles, buggies, in wheelbarrows and on foot lined up for the shot that would lead to their dream of land. About ten thousand were Afro-Americans.

In a few hours a "vacant" land had been settled. In a year Oklahoma became a U.S., not an Indian, Territory.

One of the most daring black characters to arrive was Edwin P. McCabe, described as a "handsome man of Indian complexion." He had been elected to two terms as Kansas State Auditor only to have his fellow Republicans deny him renomination for a third term. McCabe reached Oklahoma with some concrete plans and a special vision. He wanted to transform it into a black state perhaps with himself as territorial and then state governor.

To that end, McCabe applied his considerable talents in business and politics. He believed that with proper encouragement enough southern black migrants might pour into Oklahoma to form a voting majority in each election district. To help matters along he founded the town of Langston as a headquarters for the effort. It became one of thirty black towns that mushroomed in Oklahoma between 1890 and 1910.

In his impeccable three-piece suit McCabe watched the black population rise to 137,000 by 1910. But he also saw his hopes dashed by an old foe.

From the beginning whites made it clear they would not have black people flexing their political muscles in Oklahoma. In 1890, the *Kansas City News*, under the headline "Oklahoma As a Negro State," reported whites "almost foam at the mouth whenever McCabe's name is suggested for Governor [and] also at the idea of negroes getting control. . . ." The *New York Times* reported from Oklahoma that McCabe might be "assassinated within a week" and quoted a white settler saying, "I would not give five cents for his life."

McCabe realized how futile his hope for the governorship was and concentrated on building a vigorous black

Boley's Town Council ruled one of some twenty-five to twenty-seven all-black settlements built in Oklahoma from 1890 to 1910.

Oklahoma. He organized his people in Langston for another land rush in September 1891. That day McCabe was fired on by three whites and only rescued by black citizens wielding Winchesters.

McCabe was later picked to serve in a minor state office, but left his job the day Oklahoma became a state in the Union. It was hardly the Oklahoma of opportunity he had envisioned.

Black residents tried mightily to prevent Oklahoma from becoming another segregationist southern state. They formed the Equal Rights Association, the Suffrage League, the Afro-American League, the Negro Protective League, and smaller local protest associations. Some flavor of their sentiments can be seen in the words of the Equal Rights Association of Kingfisher County meeting in convention in 1904:

We pledge ourselves to resist to the bitter end the efforts of our deadly enemies in attempting to mold a sentiment against us after the southern method.

Our deadly foes are now busy educating their children to hate us and to believe that we are low, degraded, and vicious because our skins are dark.

The march of history in the form of huge white migrations crushed the ambitious hopes of nonwhite Oklahomans. Each section of land opened to settlement led to Native Americans and Afro-Americans becoming more outnumbered.

A Federal government that had once promised Indians territorial integrity and security "forever" now forced entire native reservations into individual holdings. Unfamiliar with private property and a legal system based on it, Indians saw their lands slip into white hands. They became dispossessed from their own territory, with white speculators reaping the rewards.

Black Indians called the black newcomers to their region "state negroes." It is unclear if either black population moved toward making common cause. When three hundred black Oklahomans met in convention at Muskogee in December, 1906 they protested election of an all-white Oklahoma Constitutional Convention. But among the people who wrote this proud statement were there Afro-Americans and Black Indians united?: "In this territory, white man, red man, and black man have always lived in perfect harmony; no hideous lynchings mar the good name of the Territory; no mob violence to destroy, frighten or drive off outside investors. . . ." When these three hundred delegates pointed out that blacks numbered about "80,000, owning quite a million acres, possessing a personal and real property to the value of two million and upward," were they counting their brothers and sisters who lived among Native Americans? It is unclear.

What is clear is that Oklahoma entered the Union as the forty-sixth state, but not as a haven for people of every race. Its Black Indians could not vote and its Afro-

These Choctaw members show the racial mixture that typified the Nation.

Americans faced violence if they tried to vote. Dark citizens of the state could not sit with whites in school, public buildings, railroad cars, or elsewhere. Oklahoma became the first state to segregate telephone booths.

President Theodore Roosevelt, noted for his "Square Deal," signed the document admitting Oklahoma to statehood in November 1907. Edwin P. McCabe's vision of Oklahoma crashed to earth with a thud, but the spirited man was not finished.

Three months after statehood, McCabe went to court to challenge Oklahoma's right to segregate railroad passengers by race. He may have reasoned that a solid legal victory against segregation on trains would topple an entire discriminatory system.

Court after court ruled against McCabe, and still he carried his case forward on appeal. He sold his Oklahoma home, possibly to raise money for his legal costs, and left the state. Or perhaps he was in some danger.

Finally, in 1914, the Supreme Court ruled in the case of *E. P. McCabe, et al.* v. *Atchison, Topeka and Santa Fe Railroad Company, et al.* Segregation, it said, was legal not only on Oklahoma trains but everywhere else.

McCabe's political career, like the rights of black Oklahomans, was over. He moved to Chicago and soon slipped into poverty. He died a pauper in 1920 at age seventy. His wife managed to scrape together enough money to bring McCabe's body back to Topeka, Kansas, scene of his greatest political triumph—where he was twice elected to state office. He was interred in the presence of his wife, a white undertaker, and a gravedigger.

The year before McCabe died, seventy-six black people were lynched and twenty-five cities exploded in antiblack violence. His dream for Oklahoma might have saved some of those who lost their lives or suffered injuries.

In the years before McCabe's death, another man announced a grandiose plan to rescue black people from their enemies in the Americas. Marcus Garvey, a black Jamaican, whose ancestors had fought as maroons, proposed a massive black exodus to Africa, the ancestral homeland.

Garvey, like McCabe, had concluded Afro-Americans needed an escape hatch. But for the Jamaican there was no safe place in the United States or anywhere in the Western Hemisphere for black people. Even as black settlers had poured into Oklahoma in the 1890s at McCabe's urging, some soon decided the West was no safer than the East. One group packed their belongings and left for New York City and ships that carried them to Africa. They had come to Garvey's conclusion.

12

NO BARS
CAN HOLD
CHEROKEE BILL

When the Indian Territory became Oklahoma it lurched from a possible haven for nonwhites to another white supremacist state. More died than just a dream. The young among red and black Indians suffered the most, for their future had been shut down. In their frustration and pain they slipped off to drink a lot or sleep excessively. To avoid family quarrels that grew more frequent and bitter, some left for the open road. A few turned to a life of crime.

In their own flamboyant, perverted ways our young criminals represent the societies from which they spring. They express their communities blocked goals. This helps explain why citizens see certain crooks as the crude cutting edge of a people's justice system. They ramble along settling scores and shouting for the powerless from the cold steel of a gun barrel or knife blade.

Robin Hood became a medieval hero for Saxon peasants

154

oppressed by heartless nobles and an evil king in England. Frank and Jesse James were rural thieves whose daring holdups were judged a fair response to railroad owners who cheated western farmers. During the Great Depression, many U.S. citizens, infuriated that banks had swallowed their money, glamourized wild and selfish bank robbers.

To be Indian or African here historically has meant a twisted relationship with the law. Europeans, seeking to increase their holdings and wealth at the expense of non-whites, set all the economic and legal rules of the game. Land seizures and slavery became perfectly legal, and non-white resistance in any form became illegal. Law, the justice system, and military power protected white needs from nonwhite discontent.

From the beginning some dark people abandoned any effort to live by the law, even their own peoples' sense of justice. Called "outlaws," they took up sword and musket and became outlaws. It would be strange indeed if a brutal system produced only gracious victims, men and women who met dishonesty and injustice with a shrug, and humiliation with a smile.

From the earliest maroon resistance in the Americas, oppression and pain created evil monsters as well as intrepid heroes. Many, many times a people's politics would slip into crime. And noble figures have employed excessive violence to further a just cause. Some criminals have paused in their mayhem to defend an occasional innocent victim.

In the 1880s Dick Glass led his cattle-rustling, bootlegging desperadoes into a shooting war to protect Black Creeks victimized by Cherokee "half bloods." Then he led them back to their old ways.

In the next decade wild rampages by young Cherokee Bill and an even younger Rufus Buck gang came at a moment of deep political frustration for their kin, Black Cherokees and Creeks. One senses in their frantic rage a muddled objection to dispossessed people again being told to get out.

The Dick Glass Rustler Gang

The Indian Territory after the Civil War was host to many fugitives from justice. Criminals poured in from around the country and residents called their soil "the land of the six-shooter." In 1874 Fort Smith's *Western Independent* published this eyewitness account of life:

> We have lived in and around the Indian country since the Spring of 1834, but have never known such a state of terror. Now it is murder throughout the length and breadth of the Indian country. It has been the rendezvous of the vile and wicked from everywhere, an inviting field for murder and robbery, because it is the highway between Texas, Missouri, Kansas and Arkansas.

By the time a tall, gloomy Judge Isaac Parker arrived to build his reputation as a "hanging judge," there had been fifty or more murders without arrests within fourteen months. "There's no God west of Fort Smith," said local citizens.

One lively source of trouble since the Civilized Nations first adopted slavery was the struggle between bigoted "mixed bloods" and Black Indians. By 1878 Cherokee mixed bloods were in a shooting war against Black Creeks across their invisible border. Cherokee gunmen targeted Creek Lighthorsemen, their local police.

Cherokees galloped into Creek lands to defy police authority and fire into Creek homes. By early 1880 Creeks claimed Cherokee desperadoes had slain four and wounded six people for racial reasons. When they demanded legal action, nothing happened.

For some reason, Dick Glass, whose outlaw band ruled nearby Marshalltown, decided to help out. When two Black Creeks, implicated in stealing horses, were kidnapped and lynched on Cherokee soil, Glass leaped to action. Perhaps the two were friends or members of his gang.

On the morning of July 27, 1880, Glass led his outlaws across the border into Cherokee territory and a gunfight began. Several men on both sides were wounded and Glass was shot through the cheekbone and lost his horse to Cherokee fire.

Feelings escalated on both sides. A Cherokee court found the suspects in the Creek lynchings innocent. Rewards were posted for Dick Glass, wanted dead or alive, and he had to abandon Marshalltown and the Cherokee region.

He took up trading stolen horses in Denison, Texas, for liquor which he sold in the dry Indian Territory at high prices. There was a $300 fine for selling liquor to Native Americans, but it flowed freely anyway.

In 1882 Glass had a wild shoot-out with Creek Lighthorsemen that left him so badly wounded, he was reported dead. Later that year he was captured by a Kansas sheriff seeking the $600 reward. But Glass mysteriously escaped, probably by bribing the lawman.

At the year's end Glass was again on the trail in defense of his people, leading a column of Black Creeks in the Green Peach War against mixed bloods. Then, after two years of no news about him, Glass sent a long, curious letter to the Commissioner of Indian Affairs. He denied any criminal activity and claimed he was blamed for the evil deeds of others.

His statement was well organized, clear, and his only effort to exonerate himself from the serious charges against him:

> I have been hounded for nearly five years with a reward on me dead or alive. I have been obliged to hide . . . [and others have committed crimes] and lay it on me, knowing I dare not come forward and prove my innocense for fear someone might assassinate me, as has been done to two of my companions. . . .

Glass then said his troubles stemmed from a grudge people had against him because he was black. "Had I been an Indian," he wrote, no charges would have been placed against his good name.

No one believed Dick Glass then, and it is difficult to believe him now. He was in the business of rustling cattle and selling illegal liquor. Although he apparently tried to avoid killing people, he was little more than a desperado. Historian Kenneth W. Porter has suggested, "If Robin Hood, legendary outlaw-champion of the Saxon peasantry, ever existed as a historical character, he probably resembled Dick Glass more than he did the Robin Hoods of ballads, novels and movies."

Dick Glass died as he lived, in a hail of bullets. Carrying a wagon of whiskey into the Chickasaw Nation in 1885, his gang ran into Sam Sixkiller and two other U.S. deputy marshals. In the inevitable shoot-out Glass died of bullet wounds.

Glass, like the rest of us, would prefer to be remembered for good deeds rather than bad. But his defense of his race was a short-lived, part-time job during a long life of crime.

Cherokee Bill

Sagas of the Old West reserve a special place for the best shot, worst outlaw, and most feared gunman. Billy the Kid usually is handed one of these awards, if not all. The only photograph of this mass murderer who killed twenty-one men before he died at twenty, shows a sloppy, bucktoothed, moronic young thug. But after his death, this psychopathic thrill-killer received a new life as a heroic fantasy. When Hollywood glorified his career in horse operas, it picked handsome actors such as Robert Taylor and Paul Newman to play Billy the Kid as a good guy.

What the real Billy the Kid lacked in looks, height, and bearing, a tall, charming, and handsome Cherokee Bill had in real life. But he proved quite as lethally dangerous as his white counterpart.

Cherokee Bill was born Crawford Goldsby in 1876 to George Goldsby, sergeant in the famed U.S. Tenth Cavalry Regiment, and Ellen Beck, both Black Cherokees. With his parents at Fort Concho, Texas, he entered a world of frontier law and order.

Two years after Bill was born, turmoil struck the Goldsby home when his father was accused of permitting his black soldiers to take carbines to settle a dispute with some white Texans. To avoid trial his father disappeared. (White Texans often taunted and even shot at the very black soldiers who guarded their towns and homesteads. And furious bluecoats returned the fire when they could.)

As young Bill grew older, this incident could have nagged him with sharp questions about a justice system that drives a father from his wife and baby. Mrs. Goldsby, seeking work, moved Bill and his younger brother from one place to another. The two boys were often left without parental guidance.

But his mother did enroll her older son for three years in a Cherokee, Kansas, school and for two more years at the Carlisle Indian school in far-off Pennsylvania. When Cherokee Bill returned home at twelve, his mother was living in the Indian Territory and she was remarried to a man with whom Bill could not get along.

Left alone much of the time, the only recorded advice Bill received from his mother was, "Stand up for your rights. Don't let anybody impose on you." That would not be his problem.

The young man began to explore the rough frontier life and his Cherokee heritage. He grew into a burly, six-foot teen-ager, quick to smile and make friends, and devastatingly attractive to women. In 1894 he was eighteen and so far had managed to stay out of trouble on a lawless frontier.

But if he was sensitive to the plight of his Cherokee people, he saw their trouble was mounting. Aggressive white settlers gobbled up Indian lands as fast as the U.S. government seized or bought them. In 1893 Cherokees were pushed into the process of losing their best lands and settling for payments of $265.70 each.

These payments began on June 4, 1894, and by this time, Cherokee Bill was on a rampage that made him number one on the U.S. marshal's "wanted list." Rewards for him totaled a staggering $1,300.

Cherokee Bill's life of crime began at a dance with a fistfight with black Jake Lewis. Thrashed in a fair fight, Bill came roaring back two days later, guns blazing and put two bullets in Lewis. He then fled to the hill country and joined the Jim and Bill Cook outlaw band. When a posse attacked their hideout, Cherokee Bill picked off one posseman. He had his first notch.

From that point on Cherokee Bill acted as though he knew he was destined to die in two years and wanted to kill as many men as he could. He murdered a barber during a bank holdup and then formed his own band. Then he wiped out a station agent in Nowata, a conductor on a train near Fort Gibson, and an unarmed onlooker during a post-office holdup at Lenapah. Because the man was a prominent citizen, this last senseless slaying proved to be his undoing.

Cherokee Bill was often protected from harm by loyal friends and a violent reputation. Lawmen who pursued him, hearing of his fast six-shooter action, kept a safe distance and avoided engaging him in battle. Because he was on good terms with Cherokees, Creeks, and Seminoles, he moved easily through their villages and lands, something his pursuers often could not do.

In time Cherokee Bill's crimes became so infamous and documented that investigators stopped collecting evidence. The problem was catching him.

Cherokee Bill and the Bill Cook gang paused in their criminal careers to try to collect their $265.70 government share for confiscated Cherokee lands. They realized their appearance in Tahlequah to collect the money would lead to a shoot-out. Instead they wrote out their money orders and sent them along with Effie Crittendon, a friend. She was handed the money but then followed back to the Cook hideout by lawmen seeking the desperadoes.

A gunfight began and when the smoke had cleared, Jim Cook had been wounded and captured. But Bill Cook and Cherokee Bill had escaped.

With long black hair falling to his shoulders and a smile on his face, the witty, handsome young man cheerfully rode off to further crimes. When not busy robbing people, he was known for his storytelling abilities, singing of ditties, and dancing of jigs. A white rancher who spent a day with him found Cherokee Bill "as full of life and the joy of living as ever passed this way."

Cherokee Bill captured by black and white deputies.

Women not only found him alluring, but provided him with places to hide. But a Black Cherokee girlfriend, Maggie Glass, was the cause of his capture. She invited him over one night along with her kin, Ike Rogers, who was a U.S. deputy marshal. When Rogers tried to surprise him, the two men scuffled, Maggie watched, and Bill was finally felled with a chunk of wood.

On the way to jail, Bill broke his handcuffs and leaped from Rogers's wagon. A calm rifle convinced him to climb slowly back.

Brought before Judge Isaac Parker's court at Fort Smith under heavy guard, Cherokee Bill was still full of vigor. His presence soon attracted a large, curious crowd. "No bars can hold Cherokee," pal Bill Cook boasted.

Judge Parker heard his case, sentenced him to death for the murder of the bystander at Lenapah, and sent him down to the dank cells beneath the courthouse. His lawyer immediately filed an appeal to the Supreme Court for a new trial. The outlaw's own appeal, perhaps to his mother, got a smuggled six-gun into his cell. He broke out, and shooting wildly, killed one deputy and wounded others before being recaptured.

This time Judge Parker looked at the face before him and told him that in twenty-one years on the bench at Fort Smith, and after sending dozens upon dozens to the gallows, Cherokee Bill was different: "You are undoubtedly the most ferocious monster, and your record more atrocious than all the criminals who have hitherto stood before this bar."

The judge was not finished yet. He fulminated, using such phrases as "your ferocity," "bloodshed," "bloodthirsty band," "your passion for crime," and interest in "burn, pillage and destroy." Expressing his regret that he had no worse remedy than execution, he again sentenced the desperado to die, on March 17, 1896. Bill's second appeal to the Supreme Court, like the first, was rejected.

This time there was no smuggled gun, no jailbreak. No more people would die fighting Cherokee Bill or merely standing in his way. According to a local newspaper the condemned man awakened "at 6, singing and whistling." His mother accompanied her son to a gallows in a courtyard packed with one hundred enthusiastic witnesses.

Cherokee Bill, cool to the last, looked at the crowd and joked "looks like something is going to happen." Between ages eighteen and twenty he had killed a dozen men and left others wounded and bleeding. Asked if he had any last words to offer to the assembled crowd, he answered calmly "No, I came here to die—not to make a speech."

The Rufus Buck Gang

The Rufus Buck gang, a mixture of black and red Indians, killed, killed, and killed again. They apparently never claimed their deadly spree involved a racial, political, or other higher motive. There was no reason or plan behind their pathological outburst. One man claims a member announced they wanted to drive whites from Oklahoma, but offers no evidence for this.

Rufus Buck, Sam Sampson, Maoma July, Lewis and Luckey Davis all had records of minor juvenile crimes and each had been sent to jail by Judge Parker. But that was kid's stuff.

Their murder rampage of thirteen days that began on July 28, 1895, set a record. They killed more people than the famous Starr and Dalton gangs combined, and terrorized everyone in their path.

They began by murdering a Black Indian U.S. deputy marshal, John Garrett, near Okmulgee. It was said he had been keeping his detective's eye on them.

Then they started their awesome work in earnest, killing ranchers, small storekeepers, widows, farmers, and even a child. They took cash, gold watches, clothing, and boots, but theft was just an afterthought. They were enjoying themselves.

They once voted three to two to let a white victim live. Another time they shot a little black kid in the back. At the Hassan farm Rufus Buck announced "I'm Cherokee Bill's brother." Then they forced Mrs. Hassan to prepare a huge meal, ate it, and then raped her, holding her husband at bay with Winchesters. This crime and the murder of lawman Garrett would lead them to the gallows.

On a warm August day a huge posse of Black Creek police, Indians, and whites finally trapped the five young men in a cave, and after a savage gun battle, they surrendered. None of the five had suffered a wound.

Huge crowds gathered to witness their two-day trial. Five defense attorneys were assigned to defend the youths, and one admitted to the jury, "You have heard the evidence. I have nothing to say." Judge Isaac Parker sentenced the desperadoes to die on July 1, 1896. Their case was appealed to the Supreme Court but a new trial was denied.

The day before their execution a photographer appeared and captured their mood. Slouching casually, smirking a bit, none showed any remorse for their hideous crime wave. None exhibited any fear of the fate that awaited them the

The Rufus Buck gang the day before their execution: (from left) Maomi July, Sam Sampson, Rufus Buck, Luckey Davis, Lewis Davis.

next day. Except for the handcuffs holding them together, they might be mistaken for a junior high school athletic team. There is no demented look, no savage ferocity on their faces, just a few young men hanging out somewhere.

On the gallows the next day the young men were quiet, except for Luckey Davis who, spotting his sister in the crowd, shouted "Good-bye, Martha." Then with the sudden release of the trapdoors, less than a year after their thirteen-day shooting spree began, it was all over.

Citizens of every race or color agreed that Oklahoma and the Indian Territory were a little safer after the traps were sprung.

Midway between the hangings of Cherokee Bill on March 17 and the Rufus Buck gang on July 1, the same Supreme Court that had denied their appeals, spoke on a weightier matter. On May 17 it issued a landmark decision in the history of discrimination against minorities in the United States. In *Plessey* v. *Ferguson* it ruled that segregation anywhere in the country was not illegal or unconstitutional. "Separate but equal" became the law of the land, and a legal trick that lasted until the high court overturned it in 1954 in the *Brown* v. *Board of Education* decision.

This killed any last hope that emancipation might mean equal opportunity and justice for dark people. After a bloody Civil War, decades of talk, legislation, and three Constitutional Amendments promising equality and justice, a legal lid was clamped tightly over the aspirations of nonwhite people.

Perhaps there is no connection between the Supreme Court's decision and the violent careers of Cherokee Bill and the Rufus Buck gang—just a coincidence of time. But maybe young Black Indians might have seen it coming in the government seizure and sale of their lands and the hate heaped on them by mixed bloods and whites.

Perhaps their blindly senseless criminal rampages are partly an impotent, violent scream against this last denial of any hope for dark people. The appearance at the same moment in history of the most violent Black Indian outbreaks in the U.S. and the high court's decision may not be totally accidental.

Officers of the Law

For every Black Indian or black man he sent to the gallows, Judge Isaac Parker sent two or more to the Indian Territory as U.S. deputy marshals. Countless others served the Indian Nations as Lighthorsemen or local mounted police.

One of Judge Parker's earliest actions on arriving at Fort Smith in 1875 was to hire two hundred deputy marshals. Neither race nor color guided his strong hand. As a young congressmen, Parker was known as the "Indian's Best

Mounted U.S. Deputy Marshals (from left) Amos Maytubby (Indian), Zeke Miller (white), Neely Factor and Bob L. Fortune (Afro-Americans or Black Indians).

Friend." In twenty-one years as the law west of Fort Smith, he was colorblind in his war against crime.

The Indian Territory's seventy-four thousand square miles needed a steady judicial hand. Desperate communities offered outlaws asylum in exchange for "immunity" from attacks. Towns feared to have marshals spend the night lest some desperado take offense. Resisting arrest, since it only cost a felon one more year in jail, was common.

From this turbulent land Judge Parker selected a host of dark-skinned deputy marshals: John Garrett, Bill Colbert, Robert Love, John Joss, Eugene Walker, Dick Roebuck, Ike Rogers, Morgan Tucker, Grant Johnson, Bob Fortune, Neely Factor, and Bass Reaves. Lawmen started at $500 or less a year, but could earn extra money on bounties. They could also end up dead.

Judge Parker and his deputies tried to enforce the law with an even hand. But Federal officials, from the Supreme Court and the president down, sought an Indian Territory safe for white pioneers and business people. The lives and concerns of nonwhites hardly mattered. Speaking about Native Americans at this time, T. J. Morgan, a Commissioner of Indian Affairs, put the issue bluntly: "We ask them to recognize that we are the better race; that our God is the true God; that our civilization is the better; that our manners and customs are superior."

The best known of Judge Parker's black deputy marshals, Bass Reaves, served the court from his arrival at Fort Smith until Oklahoma entered the Union in 1907. Reaves rode off for thirty-seven years to enforce the law, and only one man, Hellubee Smith, ever slipped through the nets he cast.

Reaves claimed he used clever disguises and detective skills and avoided shoot-outs. However, he admitted killing fourteen men, those that drew on him first. He survived lawless frontier years. A button was shot off his shirt, a belt was shot in two, his hat brim was shot off, and his horse's bridle reins were sliced by bullets.

Bass Reaves, Deputy Marshal under Judge Isaac Parker.

But Reaves was never wounded. For a lawman sitting on his favorite sorrel horse in a dangerous land, that was more than miraculous. It was downright lucky. Reaves also had a reputation for speaking Native American languages and studying their ways of life.

A six-gun, a disguise or two, a fast steed, and a perceptive understanding of the communities he served, made Bass Reaves's career a successful one. His story is an Oklahoma legend.

13

THE GREATEST
SWEAT AND DIRT
COWBOY
THAT EVER LIVED

Imagine a western novel or movie opening with a scene
showing black cowboys hard at work on the Texas plains.
Since this scene does not square with a traditional picture
of the West, we have never seen it. Yet thousands upon
thousands of black people labored on the broad plains of
Texas before, during, and decades after the Civil War.
Thousands became cowhands.

Some arrived when Texas was still part of Mexico and
took part in the battles that gave birth to the Lone Star
Republic. Others came to Texas later, driven by their
masters in huge caravans as the Union Army marched
through the South. Briefly during the Civil War Texas was
a place where slaveholders could safely hide their slaves.
Then Texas became free.

The black cowboys remained. "I doubt if Texas has ever
seen finer cowboys than those black men," recalled Nan

Alverson, whose father had owned slaves near Fort Worth. They had been roping and branding cattle long before they were free.

After the war the average trail crew of eleven that drove cattle up the Chisolm Trail had two or three black men. Eight thousand black cowpunchers helped shape a tradition as American as Thanksgiving and apple pie. For the usual $30 a month and grub they rode the wilderness trails and took their chances with flooding rivers, wild animals, and sudden storms.

They just never had a chance to gallop across the pages of history books or Hollywood and TV movies of the Old West.

Cowboys and Indians

As Native Americans fought their last-ditch battle for survival on the western plains, armed white cowboys symbolized their advancing enemy. The black cowhand with a Stetson hat, leather saddle, and jeans was seen as no less a foe.

Some tried to prove otherwise. Black riders did team up with Indians in various bands. In 1868 a wagon train in Stephens County, Texas, was attacked by an outfit of thirty-one Indians, two Mexicans, and two black men. "Their main leader," reported one white, "was a big negro." In the same region a black man named Cato commanded twenty-five Commanches. When they besieged the Ledbetter Salt Works, Cato was wounded and his raiders driven off.

The next year dozens of Texas citizens near Fort Belknap fought off a large group of Indians commanded by a black man. He issued his orders from a large rock out of rifle range and, after four hours of fighting, ordered his men back with a bugle call. In 1874 a Black Commanche under Quannah Parker led Kiowas, Cheyenne, Apache, and Commanche against white buffalo hunters in northwestern Texas.

These reports continued to come out of Texas throughout the late 1860s and 1870s. In 1889 a white Texan summarized his frontier experience in these words: "Very fre-

Jess (right) shown with Victorio's Apaches.

quently runaway negroes would join the Indians and render valuable assistance in stealing and fighting." Even if this Texan exaggerated, he is describing a relationship with Indians that whites on the frontier failed to develop.

Nat Love, the only black cowhand to write a full-length autobiography, ran into a Black Indian Nation in 1876 at Yellow Horse Canyon. In his account, he single-handedly battled a dozen native warriors from Yellow Dog's band. Finally, he was knocked unconscious and brought to their village.

They took good care of him, he believed, "because I had proved myself a brave man, and all savages admire a brave man." He added this description of the nation: "Then Yellow Dog's tribe was composed largely of half-breeds, and there was a large percentage of colored blood in the tribe, and I was a colored man they wanted to keep me, as they thought I was too good a man to die."

Nat Love rode all the western trails convinced Indians were "evil redskins" bent on "terrorizing the settlers . . . defying the government." He accepted the idea that "the only good Indian is a dead Indian." After a fatal shoot-out he and his buddies had with Native Americans, he reported, "we had the satisfaction of knowing we had made several good Indians out of bad ones."

The winds of racial hatred had never stopped and were again swiftly sweeping the land. Few cowhands of any color voiced any concern about the white massacres of Indian villages being carried out routinely during these years.

Slavery in the South had been wiped out only to return as segregation and sharecropping. The dark men, women, and children caught in the southern net also provoked little white concern.

A History of Aid and Comfort

More than a few significant black figures have expressed their identification with Native Americans, or fought for their rights. In 1852 Martin R. Delany, the father of black nationalism in the United States, paused in a denunciation of slavery to say of Indians: "We are identical as the subject of American wrongs, outrages and oppression, and therefore one in interest." He returned to this topic in 1859 in his famous and only novel, *Blake*, and devoted a chapter to discussing how both races might combat the common foe.

Perhaps the most stinging assault on the U.S. government's genocidal policy toward Indians came from Senator B. K. Bruce of Mississippi, a former runaway slave. On April 7, 1880, Senator Bruce stood up and told his Senate colleagues exactly how United States actions had made Indians fugitives and vagabonds in their own land. He got right to the point:

> Our Indian policy and administration seem to me to have been inspired and controlled by a stern selfishness, with a few honorable exceptions. Indian treaties have generally been made as the condition and instrument of acquiring the valuable territory occupied by the several Indian nations, and have been changed and revised from time to time as it became desirable that the steadily growing, irrepressible white races should secure more room for their growth and more lands for their occupancy; and war, bounties, and beads have been used . . . for the purpose of temporary peace and security for the whites, and as the preliminary to further aggressions upon the red man's lands, with the ultimate view of his expulsion and extinction from the continent.

Except for Native Americans, no U.S. citizen had ever placed the blame that plainly before. The senator's final plea was to "save and not destroy these people," who stood in the path of the U.S. government and its citizens. It is doubtful that many in the country listened to his troubling words.

However, by this time black people at Hampton Institute had opened their doors to a hundred Native Americans. An eager young ex-slave, Booker T. Washington, was placed in charge of a project to educate Indians in the ways of a new civilization.

Washington described the experiment in his autobiography, *Up From Slavery*:

> On going to Hampton, I took up my residence in a building with about seventy-five Indian youth. I was the only person in the building who was not a member of their race. . . .

I found that they were like any other human beings; that
they responded to kind treatment and resented ill-treatment.
They were continually planning to do something that would
add to my happinenss and comfort. The things they dis-
liked most, I think, were to have their long hair cut, to
give up wearing their blankets, and to cease smoking. . . .

It was a constant delight to me to note the interest which
the colored students took in trying to help the Indians in
every possible way. There were a few of the colored students who felt that the Indians ought not to be admitted to
Hampton, but they were in a minority. Whenever they were
asked to do so, the Negro students gladly took the Indians
as roommates, in order that they might teach them to
speak English and to acquire civilized habits.

I have often wondered if there was a white institution in
this country whose students would have welcomed the
incoming of more than a hundred companions of another
race in the cordial way that these black students at Hampton welcomed the red ones. . . .

When Mr. Washington took one of his Indian students
to Washington, D.C., the two experienced a strange color
line. Aboard the steamboat the Indian was admitted to the
dining room, and Washington was not. In the nation's
capital a hotel manager rented a room to the student, but
not to his teacher.

The Buffalo Soldiers

After the Civil War, U.S. policy was brought forcefully home
to Native Americans on the bayonets of U.S. infantry and
cavalry regiments assigned to the frontier. For the first time,
officially, this included black men, the Ninth and Tenth
Cavalry and the Twenty-fourth and Twenty-fifth Infantry
Regiments, "U.S. Colored Troops."

There is a painful irony that these intrepid black soldiers
took part in the final defeat of Native Americans, the first
victims of racism in the Americas. But take part they did,
and proudly, in the last Indian wars. Because their short
curly hair was similar to that on the buffalo's neck, Indians

Frederic Remington, the famous artist, sketched this meeting of two races when he accompanied the buffalo soldiers of the Tenth Cavalry Regiment in 1888.

called them "buffalo soldiers," and the name stuck. They marched forth to carry out the orders of their white officers and their government in Washington whose policies made peace impossible.

As the buffalo soldiers dutifully brought a white version of law and order to the frontier, they earned the respect of every military friend and foe they encountered. They guarded railroad and telegraph lines, stagecoaches and arms shipments, towns and homesteads, whites and Indians.

They moved Indian families and nations from one location to another and rode after those who left reservations to seek some freedom or merely to forage for food for starving people. From the Canadian border to the Rio Grande, from St. Louis to the Rockies and into California, the buffalo soldiers rolled up an impressive record.

Their desertion rate was the lowest in the frontier army

though their posts were often in the most remote, God-forsaken places. This was a time when more than a third of white enlisted men went A.W.O.L. each year. In 1876, for example, the white Seventh Cavalry had 72 deserters, the Third had 170, and the Fifth had 224, but the black Ninth only had 6 deserters and the Tenth 18.

As black men in a white man's army, they were subject to unusually harsh discipline, bigoted officers, and poor food and recreational facilities. The Tenth regimental standard was homemade, tattered, and worn—unlike the silk-embroidered banner supplied by headquarters to white units.

Yet their morale was high and some white officers were proud to lead so brave a military force. For scouts they employed such frontier legends as Kit Carson, Wild Bill Hickok, and the Seminole Negro Indian Scouts.

Black troopers, including those with Black Indian ancestry, operated under orders that often had them viewing Native Americans through the gunsights of their ready carbines. Eleven black soldiers earned the Congressional Medal of Honor in combat against Utes, Apaches, Commanches. The first of the eleven, Corporal Emmanuel Stance, a short ex-slave serving in Company F, Ninth Cavalry, had five encounters with Plains Nations in two years. He behaved with such valor and calmness that he won unstinting praise from his white commander along with his country's highest military decoration.

In an age that offered black men few decent, manly jobs, military life appealed to these recruits. Many had served their country during the Civil War. There is little evidence that these men disagreed with their government's genocidal policies toward Native Americans. And they certainly carried out all orders.

Artist Frederic Remington, who traveled with the Tenth Cavalry in Arizona, found them "charming men with whom to serve." He also reported to a white reading public that thought of blacks as meek, fearful, clownish people, that they were truly fearless, determined, and willing killers.

These soldiers lived through adventures rich in irony. They never knew when they might be ambushed not just by the foes they faced in the field, but by the very white townspeople they protected. For merely entering some towns or saloons, particularly in Texas, they became embroiled in shoot-outs or became targets for cowardly snipers.

One Texas citizen murdered a black trooper, killed the two black cavalrymen who came to arrest him, and then was found not guilty by a jury of his white peers. At times animosity toward bluecoats in Texas was so vicious that black and white U.S. soldiers united to defend themselves from those they were guarding. Soldiering had lost its Civil War glamour and had not yet picked up its Hollywood frontier-movie, patriotic gloss.

In 1890 black troopers were summoned to assist in the suppression of the last Indian uprising, the Ghost Dance Rebellion. Really a Sioux religious revival and prayer for survival, it managed to terrify local whites.

The U.S. Army command ordered in its troops. After surrounding 350 Sioux at Wounded Knee, the Seventh Cavalry opened fire on innocent men, women, and children. One of the fifty survivors of the massacre recalled, "We tried to run but they shot us like we were buffalo."

Black troops were not involved in the slaughter, but the Ninth Cavalry had been assigned to herding the Ghost Dancers together. To celebrate their part in the action, a Ninth Cavalry cavalryman wrote a ballad that ended with the lines:

> The Red Skins heard the Ninth was near
> And fled in great dismay.

The ironic nature of the black military legacy on the frontier was sharply etched in the life and death of Isaiah Dorman, a Black Sioux, who fought and died with George Custer at the Little Big Horn.

Dorman had worked for the army for many years and was considered "faithful and reliable in every trust." He was fluent in Sioux languages, married to a Santee Sioux woman, and had become good friends with Chief Sitting Bull. And there he was riding with Custer toward the Little Big Horn and immortality on June 25, 1876.

When the Seventh Cavalry plunged into the trap, a badly

wounded Dorman survived the battle. Sitting Bull report-
edly approached the wounded Black Sioux and said to his
men, "Don't kill that man, he's a friend of mine." Sitting
Bull gave Dorman a drink of water from his buffalo horn,
and then Dorman died.

The Last Frontier

White frontiersman Andrew Davis wrote, "It was believed
that Indians never killed Negroes—that the worst they did
to them was to take them prisoner. It was not oftcn they did
that." His optimistic view is not consistent with known facts.
Members of the two races did shoot at and kill each other,
and blacks were captured by Native Americans.

But his evaluation highlights a basic truth when it empha-
sizes that there was something very different in the relationship between the two dark races, than the one either of
them had with whites. However, life on the last frontier
could be violent and short for anyone.

Evidence of this Old West Black Indian relationship is
preserved in frontier documents and captured in the flash of
the camera's eye. This startling new device had arrived in
the West by the 1870s and 1880s—with its puff of white
smoke—to capture westerners in frozen frames for all time.

Our Black Indian tale of the last frontier ends with five
people seeking something they considered vital to their
lives. Britton Johnson was searching for his kidnapped
family. Isom Dart was seeking his love. Jim and Kitty Cloud
Taylor sought each other and the happiness of marriage.
Bill Pickett was trying to develop his cowhand skills so he
could feed his large family.

Britton Johnson's fascinating saga began before the Civil
War when "Brit" was known as one of the best shots on
the Texas frontier. He was described as "a shining jet black
negro of splendid physique" and lived with his wife and
four children in a white settlement in Young County, Texas.

In October 1864, when Johnson may still have been a
slave, Commanche and Kiowa raiders besieged his settlement. They killed some people, including his son, and galloped off with several women and children, including his

wife and his three other children. Johnson persuaded his fellow villagers that he could bring back the prisoners, and he set off alone on this mission.

His effort was a success. One story holds that he entered the Indian villages and then helped the prisoners to escape. Another story states that Johnson negotiated with the Kiowas and Commanches to win their release, and this was a long and complicated process.

Matthew Braun, a western novelist, tells this story in *Black Fox*, in words he claims are "essentially true and accurate in detail." Braun takes the brave black man through a series of harrowing contests and encounters that finally convince the Kiowas and Commanches to release their black and white captives to Johnson in exchange for horses and ponies. It is a rousing, well-told yarn and restores to this unsung hero, states Braun, "his audacity and fearlessness . . . as real as any to emerge from Western folklore."

Unfortunately for Johnson, this was not his last perilous encounter with Plains Nations. In January 1871, Johnson and three other black cowpunchers were hauling supplies on the Butterfield Trail to the Johnson family home near Fort Griffin. Suddenly twenty-five Commanches rode into view and a sharp gunfight on the broad plains soon became a life-and-death struggle.

Brit Johnson took charge of the cowhands' defense, ordering them to kill their horses and use their bodies for breastworks. The Commanches charged again and again, firing and riding toward and over the men sprawled out behind their horses. The bitter battle finally took the life of every cowhand but Johnson. He gathered up the rifles of his fallen buddies, quickly loaded them, and poured a steady fire into the attackers.

But this time Johnson's cunning, accuracy, and courage were not enough. He had fired 173 shots—the number of empty cartridges found near him—when he was cut down by enemy bullets. Possibly infuriated it took so long to slay their opponent, the Indians mutilated his body and killed his dog. "A man of heroic qualities," said one of his neighbors, had died.

Not death but love and violence entered the life of famed

black cattle rustler Isom Dart in the person of an attractive
Shoshone woman named Tickup and her daughter Mincy,
nine. Amiable, likable Dart thought it was love at first
sight, and he took in the pair who were fleeing Tickup's
mean Ute husband, Pony Beater. He drank a lot, beat up
his wife and her daughter and then fell asleep. When he had
done that once too often the two escaped.

Dart, with the two under his protection, left to avoid a
confrontation with the enraged husband. But Pony Beater
tracked them down and caught them by surprise. He had
Tickup bind Dart with leather thongs and then took off with
his family and Dart's possessions.

The first night on the trail Pony Beater drank, beat up
mother and daughter, and dropped off to sleep. He never
woke up. Tickup slit his throat, gathered up Mincy, and
headed back home to Idaho. There she hoped to find some
peace.

Meanwhile Dart freed himself and tracked down his new
family. He arrived in Idaho to find Tickup already had a
new Indian husband. Enraged, he charged at and was about
to murder the man when Tickup, ever resourceful, clobbered Dart with a stone axe so hard she almost severed
his ear.

Dart decided romance was not for him and returned to
Brown's Park, Colorado, and a rustler's life. He became
"the best bronco rider who ever threw a leg over a horse,"
according to one friend. He also became a target for bounty
hunter Tom Horn. At the age of fifty-one Dart was shot in
the back by Horn for the reward.

Compared with Dart, John Taylor was far more successful
with life, love, and Ute Indians. His story appears in three
frontier photographs. The first shows Taylor proudly posing
with a Ute friend. The next shows Taylor on his wedding
day in 1894 when he married Kitty Cloud of the Ute
Nation. Taylor is on the ground in his wedding suit, Utes
to the right and left of him with spears and rifles poised at
his heart. It looks as though Taylor is about to die. The
photograph captures a menacing moment.

But a closer look reveals that Taylor is lying on a blanket.

John Taylor and a Ute friend.

Even his neat white hat rests on the blanket. This is clearly a posed photograph. Everyone is having some fun making it seem John Taylor is about to leave this earth at the hands of the Utes.

The last photograph, taken some time later, shows Kitty Cloud Taylor, her sister, and their babies. It is clear that Mrs. Taylor's child has African as well as Ute features. The three pictures add up to a tale of love, marriage, and

Above:
In 1894, John Taylor married Ute Kitty Cloud and had his picture taken.

Right:
Kitty Cloud Taylor (standing right), her sister, and their children.

family. They also personalize a long racial friendship being continued by two people in love.

"The Bull Dogger"

In many ways the exciting saga of Bill Pickett tells us what happened to Black Indians as the last frontier entered the twentieth century. Pickett was born in 1870, the second of thirteen children, to Black Cherokees in Oklahoma.

After completing the fifth grade, Pickett left the dull confines of a frontier classroom for the wild life of the range. He landed a job as a ranch hand and developed his roping and riding skills. But Bill Pickett wanted something more of life.

He found it among the animals he tended. Some people say that when he was only ten, Pickett began to practice a technique for holding calves quiet at branding time.

Others say he began his startling skill later in Texas brush country where roping a steer was difficult if not impossible. What Pickett did was to create a cowhand technique for holding cattle that required delicate coordination, great strength, and pure macho guts.

It is called "bulldogging" or "steer-wrestling" and became the most famous cowboy sport. Pickett would race his horse Spradley after a steer and leap out of the saddle onto the animal's back. Grabbing a horn in each hand, he began the hard part. He twisted the horns until the beast's face turned upward and the huge animal fell over on its side. Rider and steer skidded to a halt in a cloud of dust.

For a final touch, Pickett sunk his teeth into the steer's upper lip or nose and let go with his hands. The startled beast lay still, shocked someone was biting its nose or lip. Everyone watching was amazed that the cowhand's only grip on the big animal was white teeth clamped onto a lip or nose.

Pickett had a wife and eventually nine children to feed. To provide for his family, he landed a job with the huge 101 Ranch in Oklahoma run by the Miller brothers. Zack Miller hired the two hundred best cowhands he could find for his ranch and rodeo. His men won so many prizes they were soon barred from local cowboy competition.

Miller took his rodeo on the road, and they entertained in Mexico City, London, New York, and in Argentina and Canada. Everywhere their featured act was Bill Pickett's bull-dogging. Billed as the "Dusky Demon" or the "Wonderful Colored Cowboy," Pickett's daring act drew the applause and admiration of young and old, cowboy or city slicker.

Pickett's five foot six, 145-pound frame swept through his bulldogging feat with the agility of a ballet dancer. He never appeared to get scratched. His other ranching talents were such that Zack Miller called Pickett "the greatest sweat and dirt cowboy that ever lived, bar none." That lofty title may still hold.

At one time or another in his rodeo career Pickett had the assistance of two other 101 cowhands destined to win fame and fortune—Tom Mix and Will Rogers. Back then

Bill Pickett on Spradley about to begin his rodeo routine.

they were just beginners who assisted the Dusky Demon in his famous act.

In his later years Pickett made two silent films. One was a black cowhand mystery movie. The other, called *The Bull-Dogger*, demonstrated his steer-wrestling artistry. Sadly, no copy of either can be found.

Pickett died in 1932, after a stallion he had tried to rope while on foot turned on him. From coast to coast he was remembered, and in New York comedian and actor Will Rogers wrote to the *New York Times* about his brave buddy. He told how Pickett had created a sport that brought

Part of the 101 Ranch rodeo crew shows white, black, and red men and women. Note Pickett seated third from the right, Will Rogers second person to his left in white, and Tom Mix second person to Roger's left, also in white.

ranch and cowpuncher life to millions of people who had never been out West.

Pickett's enduring legacy is that he single-handedly invented a sport as challenging and rough as the American outdoors. He demonstrated that one man with courage and stamina can overcome dangerous beasts.

Aboard his favorite horse, Spradley, Bill Pickett rode into the twentieth century. He had invented and mastered a perilous technique for handling steers and turned his creation into a rodeo performance. He loped in casually, as was his style, wearing his talents like comfortable western jeans. He appeared to perform his miraculous act effortlessly.

Bill Pickett's life brings our story of Black Indians to a close. He began life in the last century as a ranch hand with a large family to feed, and ended up in this one as a talented cowhand and cherished performer.

With his masterful skills, Pickett won fame and a decent living. But he never achieved in his lifetime the renown and riches of his two assistants, Tom Mix and Will Rogers. He made a journey from rural to urban life, and counted on a white world for his livelihood. It offered even Bill Pickett limited opportunities.

This poster, possibly dating from 1914, advertises the five-reel silent movie The Bull-Dogger *that featured the "Dusky Demon."*

ACKNOWLEDGMENTS

This project grew from a lingering fascination with the pioneer research that was begun by Professor Kenneth Wiggins Porter when Herbert Hoover sat as our Great White Father in the White House. As an editor for Arno Press/New York Times, I was able to have Professor Porter select his best articles for and edit *The Negro on the American Frontier* (1971). After some minor skirmishes with the subject in my *The Black West* (1971) and *Black People Who Made the Old West* (1977) in 1977, I also tried to summarize some Black Indian history in a short *Freedomways* article. After Professor Porter's death in July, 1981, Mrs. Annette Porter made me curator of her husband's uncompleted manuscripts (now housed at the Schomburg Center for Black Culture in New York City) and my interest mounted.

Along the way I have benefited enormously from research offered by doctoral candidate Joseph Opala, who shared valuable data with me on the African Seminoles; work with Professor Earl Davis of the New York University's Afro-American Studies Center, Marcia White of the American Museum of Natural History in New York City, and (as always) Sara Dunlop Jackson of the National Archives in Washington, D.C.; and by discussions with Dr. John Hope Franklin, and Ernest Kaiser of the Schomburg Center for Research in Black Culture, William Miles, Charles Fuller, Jean Carey Bond, George Tooks, Warren Halliburton, Tony Brown, Esther and James Jackson, and Charlayne Haynes.

The direct impetus for this volume came from challenging discussions with audiences at three lively forums provided by Marcia White at New York's American Museum of Natural History. Here was a case of a lecturer learning more from the audience than they learned from him. Thank you Marcia White and audiences.

My researchers included Rosalee Hamilton, Erika Lieber and my patient proof-reader was Laurie Lehman.

BIBLIOGRAPHY

Braun, Matthew. *Black Fox* (Greenwich, Ct., 1972) is a fictionalized account of the exciting adventures of Britton Johnson's encounter with Kiowas and Commanches in 1864.

Belous, Russel E., ed. *America's Black Heritage* (Los Angeles, 1969) tells the tale of early African and Indian founders of Los Angeles.

Bontemps, Arna, and Jack Conroy. *Anyplace But Here* (New York, 1966) has chapters on Du Sable and Beckwourth.

Davidson, David M. "Negro Slave Control and Resistance in Colonial Mexico, 1519–1650," *Hispanic American Historical Review,* Vol. 46, No. 3 (August 1966).

Debo, Angie. *A History of the Indians of the United States* (Norman, Okla., 1970) is an excellent summary history of Native American Nations that includes some material on black members.

Durham, Philip, and Everett L. Jones, *The Adventures of the Negro Cowboys* (New York, 1969) discusses black cowhands of the last frontier and particularly Cherokee Bill and Bill

Pickett. It is written for students and includes photographs.

Ellison, Mary. "Black Perceptions and Red Images," *Phylon* XLIV, #1, 44–45.

Forbes, Jack D. *Black Africans and Native Americans* (London, 1988) is a scholarly survey of bi-racial contacts.

Foreman, Grant. *The Five Civilized Tribes* (Norman, Okla., reprinted 1977) tells the story of the major Indian Nations after they were driven from their homes in the East to Oklahoma.

Foster, Laurence. *Negro Indian Relations in the Southeast* (Philadelphia, 1935) is a doctoral thesis which includes historical and field work data on Seminoles in Oklahoma, Texas, and Mexico.

Foster, Laurence. "Negro Indian Relationships in the Southwest." Ph.d. Dissertation, University of Pennsylvania, 1935 (copy in author's possession).

Hall, Gwendolyn Midlo. *Africans in Colonial Louisiana* (Baton Rouge, 1992) is the first thorough study of resistance to Spanish and French rule by Indians and Africans in Louisiana.

Katz, William Loren. *Breaking the Chains: African American Slave Resistance* (New York, 1990). Several chapters detail resistance by enslaved Indians and Africans.

Katz, William Loren. *The Black West, A Pictorial History* (New York, 1996, Simon & Schuster edition, revised and expanded) includes new information and photographs documenting the relationship between Africans and Native Americans on New World frontiers.

Landers, Jane. *Fort Mose: A Free Black Town in Spanish Colonial Florida* (St. Augustine, Florida, 1992) is based on archaeological and historical research in Spanish records.

Leckie, William H. *The Buffalo Soldiers* (Norman, Okla., 1967) is a scholarly study detailing the role of the Buffalo Soldiers on the last frontier.

Littlefield, Daniel F., Jr. *Africans and Seminoles: From Removal to Emancipation* (Westport, 1977) is a fine documented study.

Love, Edgar F. "Negro Resistance to Spanish Rule in Colonial Mexico," *Journal of Negro History*, Vol. LII, No. 2 (April, 1967).

Love, Edgar F. "Legal Restrictions on Afro-Indian Relations in Colonial Mexico," *Journal of Negro History*, Vol. LV, No. 2 (April 1970).

Love, Nat. *The Life and Adventures of Nat Love* (New York, reprinted 1968) is the loud and proud story of a black cowhand who encountered Indians during the days of the great cattle drives.

Mulroy, Kevin. *Freedom on the Border* (Lubbock, Tex., 1993) a valuable update of research by Porter on the Black Seminoles.

Nash, Gary B. *Red, White and Black: The Peoples of Early America* (Englewood Cliffs, New Jersey, 1974).

Opala, Joseph A. *A Brief History of the Seminole Freedmen* (Austin, Tex., 1980) is a summary written for students about the Black Seminole alliance that includes photographs, maps, and a chronology.

————. "Seminole-African Relations on the Florida Frontier," *Papers in Anthropology*, Vol. 22, No. 1 (Spring 1981) examines the complicated, changing relationship between the two races within the Seminole Nation from a new scholarly perspective.

Porter, Kenneth Wiggins. *The Negro on the American Frontier* (New York, 1971) includes scholarly articles on relations between Africans and Native Americans from the earliest European explorations through the nineteenth century, with special focus on the Seminole Nation, the fur trade, and the southern U.S. before the Civil War.

Price, Richard. *First Time: The Historical Vision of an Afro-American People* (Baltimore, 1983) is an anthropological study of the Saramaka people of Surinam and their maroon history. It is the first effort at a thorough study of a maroon people who survived for centuries.

————, ed. *Maroon Societies* (New York, 1973) has scholarly articles on maroon societies in Latin America's Spanish, Portuguese, French, and Dutch colonies, including the

Republic of Palmares in Brazil.

Shirley, Glen. *Law West of Fort Smith* (New York, 1957) tells the story of Judge Isaac Parker's frontier justice in the Indian Territory, with special emphasis on Cherokee Bill and the Rufus Buck gang.

Willis, William S. "Divide and Rule: Red White and Black in the Southeast," *Journal of Negro History*, Vol. XLVIII, No. 3, (July 1963).

Winston, Sanford. "Indian Slavery in the Carolinas Region," *Journal of Negro History*, Vol. XIX, No. 4 (October, 1934).

Wright, James L. Jr. *Creeks and Seminoles* (Lincoln, Nebraska, 1986).

INDEX

Boldface indicates illustration.